SUPERMAN ADVENTURES
LEX LUTHOR, MAN OF METROPOLIS

SUPERMAN ADVENTURES
LEX LUTHOR, MAN OF METROPOLIS

RICK BURCHETT & TERRY AUSTIN collection cover artists

SUPERMAN created by **JERRY SIEGEL** and **JOE SHUSTER**
By special arrangement with the **Jerry Siegel** family

JOEY CAVALIERI
MIKE McAVENNIE
Editors - Original Series
FRANK BERRIOS
Assistant Editor - Original Series
STEVE COOK
Design Director - Books
AMIE BROCKWAY-METCALF
Publication Design
KATE DURRÉ
Publication Production

MARIE JAVINS
Editor-in-Chief, DC Comics

DANIEL CHERRY III
Senior VP - General Manager
JIM LEE
Publisher & Chief Creative Officer
DON FALLETTI
VP - Manufacturing Operations & Workflow Management
LAWRENCE GANEM
VP - Talent Services
ALISON GILL
Senior VP - Manufacturing & Operations
NICK J. NAPOLITANO
VP - Manufacturing Administration & Design
NANCY SPEARS
VP - Revenue
MICHELE R. WELLS
VP & Executive Editor, Young Reader

SUPERMAN ADVENTURES: LEX LUTHOR, MAN OF METROPOLIS

DC Comics, 2900 West Alameda Ave., Burbank, CA 91505
Printed by LSC Communications, Crawfordsville, IN, USA. 1/22/21. First Printing.
ISBN: 978-1-77950-812-6

Library of Congress Cataloging-in-Publication Data is available.

CONTENTS

LEX

LEX LUTHOR, MAN OF METROPOLIS

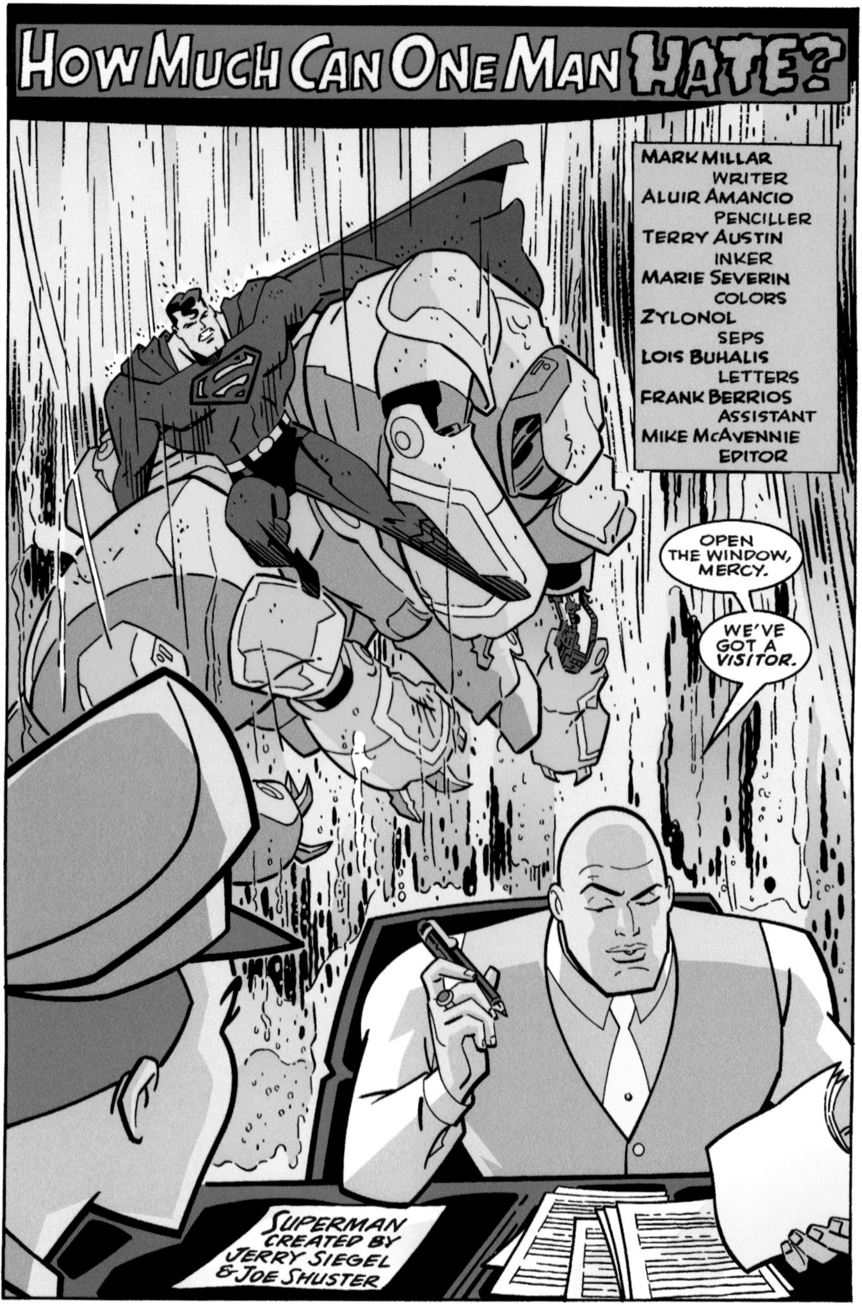

HOW MUCH CAN ONE MAN HATE?

MARK MILLAR
WRITER
ALUIR AMANCIO
PENCILLER
TERRY AUSTIN
INKER
MARIE SEVERIN
COLORS
ZYLONOL
SEPS
LOIS BUHALIS
LETTERS
FRANK BERRIOS
ASSISTANT
MIKE McAVENNIE
EDITOR

OPEN THE WINDOW, MERCY.

WE'VE GOT A *VISITOR.*

SUPERMAN CREATED BY JERRY SIEGEL & JOE SHUSTER

VRRRRRRRRR
KILLER ANDROIDS PROGRAMMED TO TRACK DOWN MY DENSE MOLECULAR STRUCTURE? A LITTLE UNINSPIRED BY EVEN *YOUR* STANDARDS, LUTHOR.
CLIK!
AS USUAL, SUPERMAN, YOU HAVE ME *COMPLETELY* AT A LOSS.
WHUDD!

STOP PLAYING GAMES, LEX. A LITTLE X-RAY INSPECTION CONFIRMS EVERY NUT AND BOLT IN THESE THINGS CAME FROM **THIS BUILDING.**
YOU MIGHT AS WELL HAVE LEFT YOUR *WALLET* AND *DRIVER'S LICENSE* AT THE SCENE OF THE CRIME.

BELIEVE ME, SUPERMAN, EVEN *YOU* WITH YOUR GREAT STRENGTH WOULD HAVE TROUBLE LIFTING *MY* WALLET.
AND AS FOR THOSE BITS AND PIECES USED TO BUILD YOUR LITTLE PLAY-MATES...

...YOU'LL FIND THEY WERE STOLEN FROM OUR WAREHOUSE BY A CRAZED EX-EMPLOYEE WITH A GRUDGE AGAINST A CERTAIN MAN OF STEEL.
CHECK THE FILES FOR YOURSELF IF YOU DON'T BELIEVE ME.

OH, I'M SURE THEY'RE ALL IN PERFECT ORDER.
WHAT'S THE MATTER, SUPERMAN? YOU'RE STARTING TO SOUND A LITTLE PARANOID. DON'T TELL ME THE JOB'S STARTING TO GET TO YOU.

STILL, THE NUMBER OF PSYCHOPATHS OUT THERE TRYING TO KILL YOU ON A DAILY BASIS MUST BE RATHER STRESSFUL. AFTER ALL, THEY ONLY HAVE TO BE LUCKY ONCE, BUT YOU HAVE TO BE LUCKY ALL THE TIME.

WHY DO YOU DO IT, LUTHOR? WHY DO YOU WASTE ALL THIS TIME AND ENERGY? IS IT THE POWERS? IS IT THAT I HAVE HAIR?
WHAT HAVE I EVER DONE TO MAKE YOU HATE ME THIS MUCH?

IF YOU HAVE TO ASK, YOU'LL NEVER KNOW.

LEXCORP
MANIAC.

HOW MUCH DID HE COST ME TODAY, MERCY?
ONLY TEN MILLION BUCKS, BOSS. A FEW HUNDRED LESS THAN THE ROBOT DUPLICATE YOU DESIGNED A FEW MONTHS AGO...

...AND A FRACTION OF THE PRICE YOU PAID FOR THE BIZARRO PROGRAM, THE GALACTIC GOLEM OR THE HAMMER OF HATE.
WE'RE ALMOST ON BUDGET FOR A CHANGE THIS MONTH.
THAT DOESN'T EXCUSE THE FACT THAT A CREATURE OF NO OBVIOUS INTELLIGENCE HAS THWARTED ME YET AGAIN, MERCY...

...OR EXPLAIN WHY THE PEOPLE OF THIS CITY ARE ERECTING A *STATUE* TO HONOR A *THING* FROM ANOTHER WORLD THIS AFTERNOON.
HOW DOES HE MAINTAIN THIS PRETENSE?

WHO WILL RID ME OF THIS TERRIBLE BEING?!
SHKREESH!

CLEANERS, VIDEO REPAIR AND A NEW BUST OF EINSTEIN FOR THE DESK.

FETCH THE CAR, MERCY. WE'VE GOT AN APPOINTMENT TO KEEP IN CENTENNIAL PARK.

ARE YOU SURE WATCHING THE MAYOR UNVEIL A STATUE OF SUPERMAN IS A SMART IDEA WHEN YOU'RE IN THIS KINDA MOOD, BOSS?
SMART IDEAS ARE HOW I STAY IN BUSINESS, MERCY...

"...BESIDES, WHAT GREATER SOURCE OF INSPIRATION FOR A NEW PLAN THAN WATCHING THEM LINE UP TO TOUCH THE HEM OF HIS CAPE?"
IT'S GETTING LATE, BOSS. EVERYONE ELSE LEFT HOURS AGO.

IS THIS STATUE REALLY SUCH A BIG DEAL? I MEAN, HOW MANY SCHOOLS AND HOSPITALS HAVE YOUR NAME ABOVE THE DOORWAY, *huh*?
ALL PAID FOR WITH MY OWN MONEY, MERCY.

THIS NEVER COST SUPERMAN A PENNY.

NEW PLAN BEGINNING TO FORM?
STUDY MY EXPRESSION AND DECIDE FOR YOURSELF, MY DEAR.
THIS IS OUR MOST PERFECT SCHEME YET.

I STILL CAN'T BELIEVE HE STOOD EVERYONE UP, Mr. KENT.
WHY WOULD SUPERMAN DISAPPOINT PEOPLE LIKE THAT?
WELL, HE'S NEVER BEEN THE TYPE TO STICK AROUND AND *WAIT* TO BE THANKED, JIMMY. I GUESS SUPERMAN JUST FINDS THIS KIND OF PUBLIC ATTENTION A LITTLE... ***UNCOMFORTABLE.***

AND WHEN DID ***YOU*** BECOME SUCH AN AUTHORITY, SMALLVILLE?
OLSEN!

WHAT ARE YOU DOING SITTING AROUND STARING INTO YOUR COFFEE BEANS WHEN TOMORROW'S FRONT PAGE IS UNFOLDING DOWNTOWN?
ORDINARY CREEP OR SUPER-CREEP, CHIEF?

DEFINITELY THE ***LATTER,*** LOIS- ***THE PARASITE'S*** CRAWLED OUT FROM WHATEVER ROCK HE WAS HIDING UNDER.
SAY, WHERED KENT GO?

GUESS THE PARASITE SURVIVED OUR LAST ENCOUNTER AFTER ALL, CAPTAIN.
ONE THING I'VE LEARNED IN THIS JOB IS THAT THE BAD GUYS *NEVER* STAY DEAD FOR LONG, SUPERMAN. WE'VE GOT HIM CORNERED DOWNSTAIRS IN THE SUBWAY STATION.
WHUMMP!
APPARENTLY NOT FOR MUCH LONGER.
BETTER KEEP YOUR BOYS BACK, MAGGIE. THIS IS GOING TO GET PRETTY ROUGH.
Um, SUPERMAN, THE PARASITE DIDN'T THROW THAT PUNCH...
...HE WAS ON THE *RECEIVING* END!
Huh?!

TAKE ALL THE PICTURES YOU WANT, BOYS AND GIRLS. JUST BE SURE TO CATCH MY BEST SIDE FOR THE LADIES.

NICE JOB, FRIEND. IT'S ALWAYS A PLEASURE TO MEET SOMEONE ELSE IN THE SAME LINE OF WORK. WHAT DO YOU CALL YOURSELF?
SUPERIOR-MAN, OF COURSE! HOW ELSE DO YOU DESCRIBE THE ONE GUY IN METROPOLIS STRONGER THAN SUPERMAN?

GET USED TO THE NAME, FOLKS. IT'S GOING TO BE EVERYWHERE ONCE I CATCH THE CROOKS THE MAN OF STEEL COULDN'T.
LOIS LANE, DAILY PLANET- ARE YOU SAYING SUPERMAN HAS A PARTNER?

Oh, NOT A PARTNER, GORGEOUS...
...A REPLACEMENT.

AFTER CAPTURING A VILLAIN SUPERMAN ALLOWED TO SLIP THROUGH HIS FINGERS, SUPERIOR-MAN HAS SINCE WOWED METROPOLIS BY SAVING THE CITY FROM THE MONSTROUS KALIBAK...

...ARRESTING THE EVER-ELUSIVE TOYMAN...

...SUBDUING TITANO, THE SUPER-APE, RECENTLY FREED FROM HIS ISLAND SANCTUARY BY ANIMAL RIGHTS ACTIVISTS...

...AND BRINGING ALMOST EVERY WANTED GOON IN METROPOLIS TO JUSTICE, DECLARING THE CITY A VIRTUAL CRIME-FREE ZONE.
IS IT ANY WONDER PEOPLE ARE SUDDENLY ASKING IF WE STILL NEED A SUPERMAN?

BUT MOST DRAMATIC OF ALL IS THE STATEMENT ABOUT TO BE MADE HERE AT THE HEADQUARTERS OF LEXCORP INTERNATIONAL...
LEX

LADIES AND GENTLEMEN, LEXCORP IS PROUD TO ANNOUNCE OUR FORMAL PARTNERSHIP WITH SUPERIOR-MAN IN LIGHT OF THE BREATHTAKING CHANGES HE'S MADE TO METROPOLIS IN SUCH A SHORT TIME.
KLIK
KLIK
FAASH!

COMBINING OUR TECHNOLOGY WITH HIS STRENGTH AND ENTHUSIASM, WE FIRMLY BELIEVE WE CAN TURN THIS CITY INTO A UTOPIA.
THE SKY IS NO LONGER THE LIMIT.
KLIK
KLIK
FAASH!

THE NEW HERO'S FANS IN METROPOLIS WERE ECSTATIC.
A PLAIN-SPEAKING ATTITUDE THAT APPEALS TO EVERYONE.
TACKLING PROBLEMS EVEN SUPERMAN DIDN'T TOUCH.
BUT ONE QUESTION STILL REMAINS:

WHO IS SUPERIOR-MAN, AND WHERE DID HE COME FROM?

MISSING
TRACKING DOWN LOST CATS WITH YOUR X-RAY VISION, SUPERMAN? TELL ME IT HASN'T COME TO **THIS**.

WHAT'S **NEXT**, BLUE-BOY? HELPING OLD LADIES CROSS THE STREET? CLEARING SNOW FROM PEOPLE'S DRIVEWAYS?
UNLIKE **YOU**, I DON'T DO THIS FOR THE PUBLICITY, FRIEND.

SO ME GRABBING ALL THOSE HEADLINES **DOESN'T** BOTHER YOU?
BEING RELEGATED TO **NUMBER TWO** ISN'T GOING TO DRIVE YOU OUT OF TOWN LIKE I FIGURED?
DREAM ON, MISTER. I'M HERE TO STAY.

WELL, IN THAT CASE, SUPERMAN, I'VE GOT A MESSAGE TO DELIVER FROM **LEX LUTHOR**...

KA-WHAM!
REST IN PEACE, FREAK!

LUTHOR? WHY IS IT --NNGH-- ALWAYS LUTHOR?

ARE YOU THE LATEST "ULTIMATE WEAPON" HE'S BUILT TO ASSASSINATE ME?

ACTUALLY, THE IDEA WAS TO REPLACE YOU, SUPERMAN.
SHOW YOU HOW HUMILIATING IT FEELS TO BE THE PEOPLE'S FAVORITE ONE MINUTE, AND OBSOLETE THE NEXT.

ARRGH!

KILLING YOU WAS JUST THE BACKUP PLAN.

THWAK!

THAT WAS KRYPTONITE-VISION, FLY-BOY. JUST ONE OF THE POWERS LUTHOR GAVE ME FOR THE NEW METROPOLIS WE PLAN TO RULE.

HE KNEW BETTER THAN ANY-ONE HOW A FLASHY NEW HERO WAS ALL IT TOOK TO MAKE THEM FORGET ALL THE GOOD WORK YOU'VE DONE.

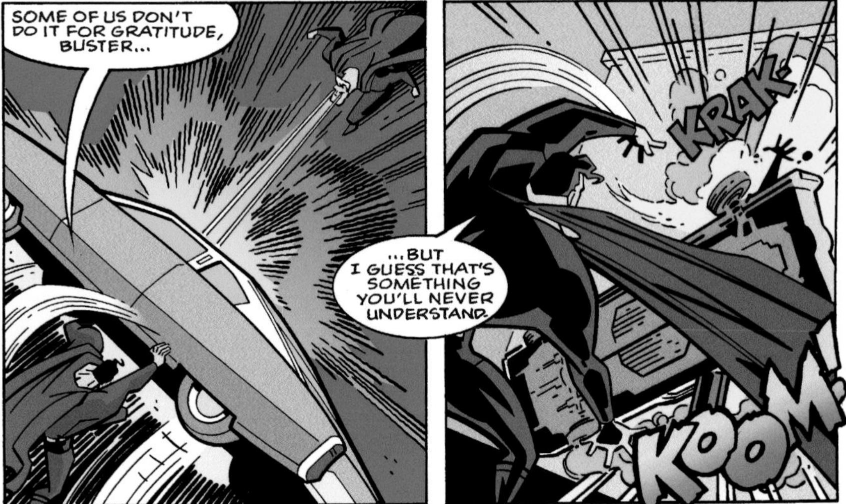

BA-BOOM!

GREAT SCOTT!
METALLO!
M-METALLO? YES, THAT'S RIGHT. JOHN CORBEN. THE KILLER WITH THE KRYPTONITE HEART. WHERE... WHERE AM I, SUPERMAN?
DID LUTHOR DO SOMETHING TO MY HEAD?

CORBEN, STAY CALM! WE CAN... AAAHH!
HE BRAINWASHED ME, DIDN'T HE?
BRAINWASHED ME INTO WORKING FOR HIM AGAIN!

THAT BALD, TREACHEROUS SLUG! MY BRAIN WAS THE ONLY THING I HAD LEFT!

NOTHING NUMBS THE TASTE BUDS LIKE THE FRIVOLOUS CHATTER OF THE COGS IN MY MACHINE, MY DEAR...
THANK THE MANAGER ON MY BEHALF FOR REMOVING THE NEARBY DINERS AND REFUNDING THEIR MONEY. INFORM HIM THAT LEX LUTHOR IS MOST SATISFIED WITH HIS BUSINESS SENSE.

IT'S BEEN A VERY PRODUCTIVE MONTH, MERCY.
SUPERMAN REPLACED AS THE HERO OF METROPOLIS, HIS SUCCESSOR UNDER MY ABSOLUTE CONTROL, AND A PURPOSE FOR METALLO, AFTER ALL.

YOU CAN TELL OMEGA SECTOR TO EXPECT A BONUS THIS MONTH.
IT ISN'T EVERY DAY OUR PEOPLE REPROGRAM A REVENGE-CHARGED SUPER-VILLAIN, HELL-BENT ON DESTROYING ME.
THAT MUST BE WORTH A FEW LEXCORP NECKTIES, AT LEAST.

K-RUNCH!

BETTER CANCEL THAT MEMO, MERCY...
THE "REVENGE-CHARGED SUPER-VILLAIN" IS BACK FOR REVENGE.
METALLO, NO!
KRUNCH!
DON'T WASTE YOUR BREATH, LEX, OLD PAL.
MY BRAINWASHING WAS REVERSED WHEN SUPERMAN BURNED OFF THAT SYNTHETIC SKIN YOU COVERED ME WITH...
CHANG!
Skrissh!
REENCH!
...NOW I'M FINALLY GOING TO MAKE YOU PAY FOR TURNING ME INTO THIS FRANKENSTEIN'S MONSTER!
BOSS! LOOK WHAT HE'S DONE TO THE CHOPPER!
I'M GOING TO MAKE YOU EAT THIS, YOU SLIME-BALL.
VERY VERY SLOWLY...

WHOKK!
WHAT THE HECK?
SUPERMAN. DON'T YOU KNOW WHEN YOU'RE BEATEN?
WHAT ARE YOU DOING WEARING THAT RIDICULOUS COSTUME?
SWEET DREAMS, METALLO.
SEE YOU IN THE CELLS WHEN WE RECONNECT YOU LATER.
OH, NO.
LEAD-LINED RADIATION SUIT FROM YOUR FRIENDS AT S.T.A.R. LABS?
CLEVER BOY, LUTHOR. RIGHT THE FIRST TIME.
YOU TWO OKAY?
CLINK

WHY SHOULDN'T WE BE?
EVERYTHING WAS UNDER MY ABSOLUTE CONTROL, SUPERMAN.

"ABSOLUTE CONTROL"?
I SAW A MAN SO CONSUMED BY HIS OWN MADNESS THAT HE ALMOST KILLED HIMSELF THIS TIME!

HOW MANY FIENDISH PLOTS AND DEATH-RAYS ARE THERE GOING TO BE, LUTHOR? HOW MANY BILLIONS OF DOLLARS ARE YOU GOING TO WASTE?

YOU WERE BLESSED WITH A BRILLIANT MIND. YOU COULD MAKE THE WORLD SUCH A WONDERFUL PLACE.

STOP WASTING YOUR LIFE TRYING TO DESTROY IT.

YOU STILL THINKING ABOUT WHAT SUPERMAN SAID, BOSS?
YES, MERCY. I'VE BEEN GIVING IT RATHER A LOT OF CONSIDERATION.
EXTRA!! SUPERIOR-MAN REVEALED AS METALLO

I'VE SPENT EIGHT BILLION DOLLARS TRYING TO DESTROY HIM IN THE LAST FINANCIAL YEAR, AND TEN HOURS EVERY DAY DEVISING DEATH-TRAPS.
WHAT HAVE I ACCOMPLISHED? ABSOLUTELY *NOTHING.*

AND NOW YOU THINK IT'S TIME TO CALL IT *QUITS?* SPEND YOUR MONEY ON SOMETHING *USEFUL?* MAYBE TAKE A LITTLE *VACATION TIME?*
AFTER THAT PATRONIZING LITTLE RANT ABOUT WHAT I SHOULD BE DOING WITH MY LIFE? *ABSOLUTELY NOT!*

NEXT YEAR'S BUDGET WILL INCREASE TO *TWENTY BILLION! SIXTEEN* HOURS EVERY DAY MUST BE DEVOTED TO HIS ABSOLUTE *NONEXISTENCE!*
A PLAN IS ALREADY BEGINNING TO FORM, MERCY...

I BELIEVE THIS IS MY MOST PERFECT SCHEME YET.
LEXCORP

YEARS AGO...
WATCHA DOIN' HIDIN' IN YOUR ROOM, LEX? WRITIN' A FANCY ITALIAN OPERA OR SOMETHIN'?
LEXCORP
IF YOU REALLY MUST KNOW, FATHER, I AM CONSTRUCTING A MODEL OF THE LEXCORP HEADQUARTERS I PLAN TO BUILD IN METROPOLIS THIRTEEN YEARS FROM NOW.
LOOK AT IT--THE TALLEST BUILDING IN ALL THE CITY. MAGNIFICENT, ISN'T IT?
WHERE'D I GO WRONG WITH YOU, BOY? WHY CAN'T YA STOP MAKIN' PLANS FOR A CHANGE AND PLAY BALL WITH OTHER KIDS SOMETIMES?
YOU'RE SEVEN YEARS OLD, FOR CRIPES' SAKE!
PRECISELY, FATHER. TIME IS MY ALLY, AND I HAVE NO INTENTION OF RESIDING IN THIS WRETCHED APARTMENT BEYOND THE AGE OF TEN.
THIS IS GOING TO BE THE HEART OF A MULTI-NATIONAL BUSINESS EMPIRE ENVIED FROM ONE END OF THE WORLD TO THE OTHER.
ONE DAY, LEX LUTHOR IS GOING TO LOOK DOWN UPON METROPOLIS...

"... AND EVERYONE IS GOING TO LOOK UP TO *ME*."
END

LEX LUTHOR, MAN OF METROPOLIS

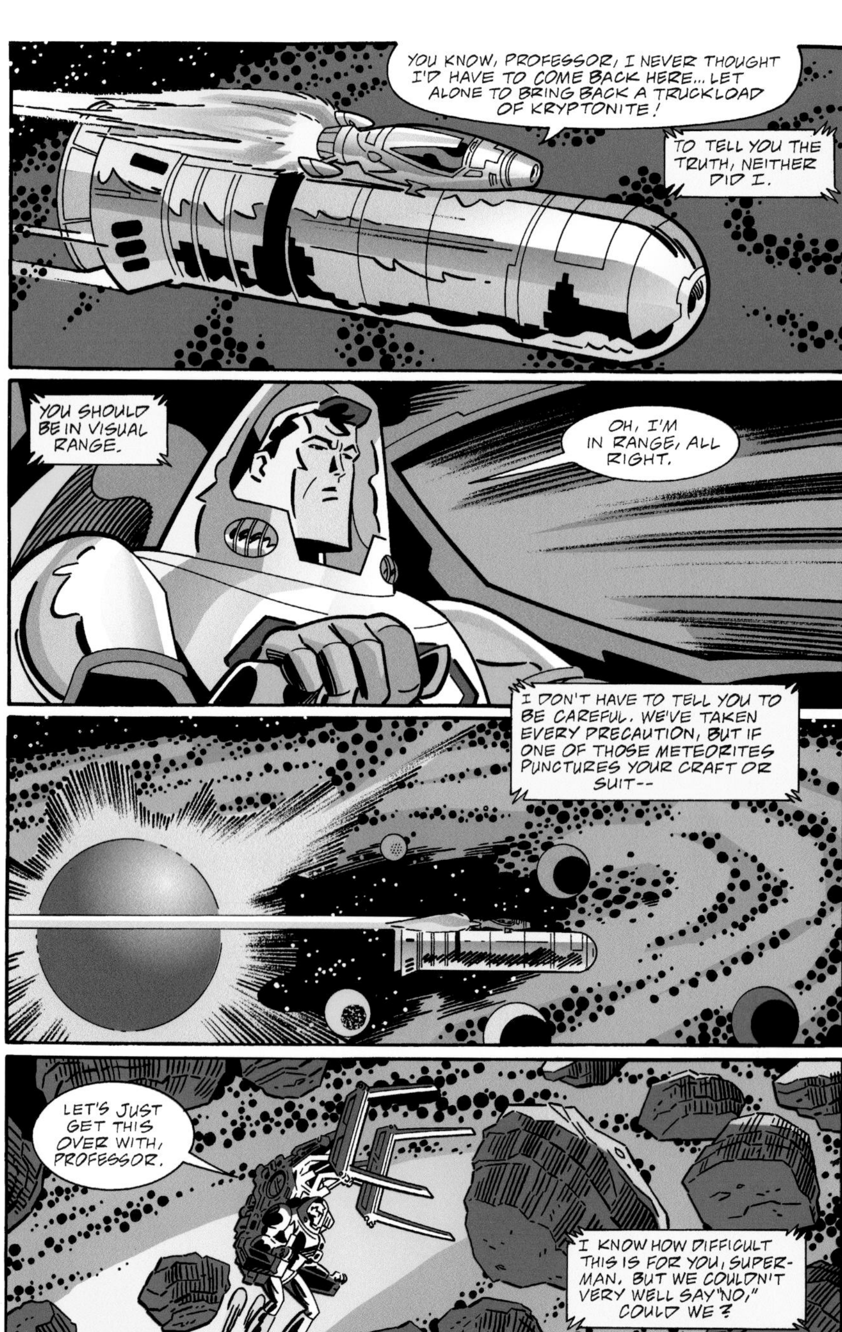
YOU KNOW, PROFESSOR, I NEVER THOUGHT I'D HAVE TO COME BACK HERE... LET ALONE TO BRING BACK A TRUCKLOAD OF KRYPTONITE!
TO TELL YOU THE TRUTH, NEITHER DID I.
YOU SHOULD BE IN VISUAL RANGE.
OH, I'M IN RANGE, ALL RIGHT.
I DON'T HAVE TO TELL YOU TO BE CAREFUL. WE'VE TAKEN EVERY PRECAUTION, BUT IF ONE OF THOSE METEORITES PUNCTURES YOUR CRAFT OR SUIT--
LET'S JUST GET THIS OVER WITH, PROFESSOR.
I KNOW HOW DIFFICULT THIS IS FOR YOU, SUPER-MAN. BUT WE COULDN'T VERY WELL SAY "NO," COULD WE?

KRYPTONITE NO MORE!
DEAN MOTTER — WRITER
ALUIR AMANCIO — PENCILLER
TERRY AUSTIN — INKER
PHIL FELIX — LETTERER
MARIE SEVERIN — COLORIST
ZYLONOL — SEPARATIONS
JOEY CAVALIERI — EDITOR
INSPIRED BY DENNIS O'NEIL, CURT SWAN AND MURPHY ANDERSON
SUPERMAN CREATED BY JERRY SIEGEL AND JOE SHUSTER
OF COURSE NOT. BUT I'M SURE HE IS ENJOYING THE FACT THAT THE ONLY MAN WHO CAN "MINE" HIS KRYPTONITE FOR HIM IS THE ONE MAN IT CAN KILL.
JUST REMEMBER, DON'T RUSH. WE NEED TO CONSERVE ENERGY. RETURNING WITH THIS AMOUNT OF CARGO WILL REQUIRE THE MAXIMUM AMOUNT OF POWER YOU AND YOUR SHIP ARE CAPABLE OF.
POWER. THAT'S WHAT THIS IS ALL ABOUT, ISN'T IT...?

KRA-AAKKK!
THAT TANKER'S LEAKING...AND LIGHTNING HAS SET THE OIL ON THE SURFACE ON FIRE!
THE HEPHAESTUS OIL FIELDS, NORTHERN PACIFIC. ONE WEEK EARLIER...
HELP! SUPERMAN!
HELP! HELP!
I'VE GOT YOU!
YOU MEN TAKE COVER--

--I'LL PULL THE SHIP A SAFE DISTANCE FROM THE FIRE!
WHILE THE NAVY GETS THE BLAZE UNDER CONTROL, I'LL SCAN THE WATER TO RESCUE OTHERS!
SOON...
THE HULL BREACH IS STABILIZED, AND THE MEN ARE ACCOUNTED FOR, THANKS TO YOU.
SHIP-TO-SHORE, SIR.
THANK YOU, SON.
HELLO, LOIS? IT'S CLARK. THERE'S NO WAY I'M GOING TO MAKE IT TO PERRY'S EMERGENCY MEETING TONIGHT.
I'LL STILL BE IN ALASKA. I THINK THE POWER COMPANIES ARE GOING TO HAVE SOME EX-PLAINING TO DO AFTER TONIGHT. I'LL FILL YOU IN LATER.
JUST MAKE MY APOLOGIES, AND PLEASE TAKE NOTES THIS TIME.
LOIS? LOIS?

DAILY PLAN
WELL, WELL...

...LOOKS LIKE THE GUEST LIST IS A LITTLE EXCLUSIVE.
OKAY. EVERYBODY'S HERE. WHAT'S THIS ALL ABOUT?

MY FRIENDS, WE ARE ON THE VERGE OF A TECHNOLOGICAL BREAKTHROUGH. ONE THAT WILL CHANGE THE VERY FACE OF CIVILIZATION.

WHY THE CLOAK-AND-DAGGER ROUTINE, LUTHOR?

THIS IS SO RADICAL THAT MANY OF MY ENEMIES--UH--COMPETITORS--WOULD STOP AT NOTHING TO ACQUIRE--OR SUPPRESS IT.

WELL, IF THIS ISN'T A PRESS CONFERENCE, LUTHOR, JUST WHAT DO YOU WANT FROM THE PLANET?
AND S.T.A.R. LABS?

LEXCORP R & D HAS DISCOVERED A NEW SOURCE OF ENERGY. A MINERAL WHICH, WHEN ENRICHED BY MY RECENTLY DEVELOPED PROCESS, MIGHT PROVIDE AN UNLIMITED, PERPETUAL SUPPLY OF POWER.
A SMALL AMOUNT WOULD GENERATE ENOUGH ELECTRICITY TO SUSTAIN GLOBAL ENERGY REQUIREMENTS INDEFINITELY.
IMPOSSIBLE!
YOU TWO EGGHEADS CAN FIGHT THIS OUT ON YOUR OWN TIME. IF YOU DON'T WANT PUBLICITY, THEN WHAT?
I NEED YOUR HELP ENLISTING...
...SUPERMAN.
GOOD LUCK...
BUT WHY SUPERMAN? WHY S.T.A.R. LABS?
YOU HAVE THE MEANS TO COLLECT THE MINERAL FROM DEEP SPACE. I AM AWARE OF SUPERMAN'S EXPEDITIONS IN THE ALIEN CRAFT YOU HAVE BEEN TESTING.
SNAP!

IN FACT, HE'S BEEN TO THE VERY SOURCE OF THIS MINERAL. THE MOTHER LODE. I BELIEVE YOU CALL IT THE ARGO ASTEROID FIELD.
SPLAT!

THIS IS CLASSIFIED! HOW DID YOU GET--?
A LEAK, PROFESSOR. DON'T WORRY. IT'S BEEN PLUGGED.
THE MINERAL IS... KRYPTONITE?!

WHAT MAKES YOU THINK THAT SUPERMAN WOULD EVEN THINK OF PUTTING THAT POISON INTO YOUR HANDS?!
I DON'T BELIEVE SUPERMAN IS SO SELFISH THAT HE WOULD DEPRIVE THE WORLD OF SAFE, CLEAN, NEARLY INFINITE ENERGY, DO YOU?
BUT IT'S LETHAL TO HIM!

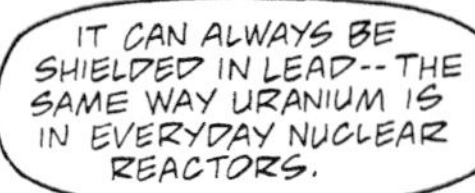
IT CAN ALWAYS BE SHIELDED IN LEAD--THE SAME WAY URANIUM IS IN EVERYDAY NUCLEAR REACTORS.

...AND ANY RADIATION LEAK WOULD ONLY BE FATAL FOR TWO PEOPLE ON THE ENTIRE PLANET!

SUPERMAN AND SUPERGIRL...

WITH PROPER SAFEGUARDS, THERE IS VIRTUALLY NO RISK.
EVEN SO, CONSIDER THE TRADEOFFS.
POLLUTION, FAMINE, TERRITORIAL DISPUTES OVER NATURAL RESOURCES, ENVIRONMENTAL DAMAGE... ALL RELICS OF THE PAST.

AND YOU WANT *US* TO CONVINCE HIM...

SUPERMAN AND I DO NOT ENJOY A VERY--AMICABLE--RELATIONSHIP. I FEAR A REQUEST FROM ME WOULD FALL ON DEAF EARS.

I UNDERSTAND HIS *HEARING* IS PRETTY GOOD...

I THINK HE WOULD *LISTEN* TO HIS FRIENDS... AND TO THE *PUBLIC*.

WHY WOULD HE *BELIEVE YOU*? WHY SHOULD WE?

ANOTHER REASON I AM APPROACHING S.T.A.R. LABS... *INDEPENDENT VERIFICATION.*

AND YOUR MOTIVES--
NOT AS PHILANTHROPIC AS HIS WOULD BE, I CONFESS. THIS IS NOT BAD FOR BUSINESS. NOT MINE, ANYWAY.
STILL, I SUPPOSE I COULD BE PERSUADED TO BE GENEROUS...
I'M ACTUALLY SWEATING, PROFESSOR. NO WAY TO WIPE IT FROM MY EYES.
JUST STAY CALM. THE SUIT IS HOLDING UP FINE AGAINST THE TOXIC EFFECTS OF THE RADIATION, BUT YOU'RE IN THE PROXIMITY OF EXTRAORDINARILY LARGE AMOUNTS OF IT. YOUR ACTIVE POWERS ARE MORE OR LESS NULLIFIED, AS WE PREDICTED.

YOU DON'T HAVE TO DO THIS, CLARK. NO ONE WOULD BLAME YOU IF YOU SAID NO. THE WORLD HAS GOTTEN ALONG FINE JUST THE WAY THINGS ARE.
YOU WEREN'T IN ALASKA... THEY HAVEN'T EVEN STARTED THE CLEANUP YET.
THERE'S NO GUARANTEE THAT IT WILL WORK ANYWAY.
YOU DON'T THINK I COULD LIVE KNOWING THERE WAS EVEN A CHANCE, DO YOU? IF IT DID WORK, I COULD DEVOTE MORE TIME TO FIGHTING EVIL AND LESS TO UNDOING CIVILIZATION'S MISTAKES.
YOU KNOW YOU COULD DIE WHETHER IT WORKS OR NOT.
THAT WOULD PUT AN END TO ALL OF YOUR EFFORTS...
I KNOW...
LET'S GO IN, JONATHAN. I'M GETTING A CHILL.
WHATEVER YOU DECIDE, CLARK, WE KNOW IT'LL BE THE RIGHT CHOICE.
OKAY, PROFESSOR. THE HOPPER IS JUST ABOUT FULL. I'M READY TO COME HOME.
DRIVE CAREFULLY.

"SINCE THE DAWN OF CIVILIZATION, MAN HAS ALWAYS REQUIRED ENERGY. WHETHER IT WAS COAL, STEAM, OIL, HYDROELECTRICITY OR THE POWER OF THE ATOM, THE TASK OF GENERATING SUCH ENERGY HAS ALWAYS PROVIDED NEW FRONTIERS FOR INDUSTRIAL MAN.

"BUT ENERGY COMES AT A PRICE. POLLUTION, TOXIC BYPRODUCTS, SAFETY HAZARDS, GREENHOUSE GASES. SOME SAY THAT PRICE CAN BE TOO HIGH. WE AT LEXCORP COULDN'T AGREE MORE.

"THAT'S WHY WE'VE SPENT YEARS DEVELOPING A TRULY ALTERNATIVE ENERGY SOURCE. SMALL AMOUNTS OF AN EXTRATERRESTRIAL ISOTOPE KNOWN AS ***KRYPTONITE*** CAN PROVIDE BILLIONS OF GIGAWATTS OF POWER, CLEANLY AND EFFICIENTLY. THIS MINERAL EXISTS IN BOUNTIFUL SUPPLY IN OUTER SPACE.

"ONCE THE ENERGY IS EXTRACTED, IT LEAVES NO WASTE TO DISPOSE OF, NO MEDICAL SIDE EFFECTS, NO RUINED LANDSCAPE OR ENDANGERED SPECIES. COULD THIS BE THE ANSWER TO ALL OF OUR ENERGY NEEDS?

"FROM ARTIFICIAL HEARTS TO MUNICIPAL POWER STATIONS, FROM POCKET CALCULATORS TO NUCLEAR SUBMARINES, POWER CAN BE AVAILABLE AND AFFORDABLE TO EVERYONE.

"THANKS TO LEXCORP, MAN NEED NO LONGER FOUL HIS ENVIRONMENT, OR STRIPMINE HIS COUNTRYSIDE. HE NEED NOT TRANSPORT PETROLEUM THROUGH WILDLIFE HABITATS, NOR FEAR THE UNINTENDED EFFECTS OF LIVING NEAR DANGEROUS POWER PLANTS."

WELCOME TO THE NEW WORLD OF ENERGY... THE WORLD OF K-POWER... COURTESY OF YOUR FRIENDS AT LEXCORP!

LADIES. GENTLEMEN. YOU'VE JUST SEEN THE PUBLIC SERVICE AD, SO I WON'T BORE YOU WITH ANY MORE TECHNO-BABBLE.

LET US SAY THAT, AFTER TODAY, NO ONE ON EARTH NEEDS TO GO WITHOUT POWER AGAIN. THE WORLD'S ENERGY PROBLEMS WILL BE A THING OF THE PAST.

TODAY A NEW DAY DAWNS.

MORE POWER TO YOU

LEXCORP

BUT I CAN'T TAKE ALL OF THE CREDIT. IN ADDITION TO MISTER BONHAM AND THE DEDICATED PERSONNEL OF LEX-CORP, A DEBT OF GRATITUDE IS OWED OUR COLLEAGUES AT S.T.A.R. LABS. PROFESSOR HAMILTON?

THANK YOU, MISTER LUTHOR. THIS IS A GREAT DAY INDEED.

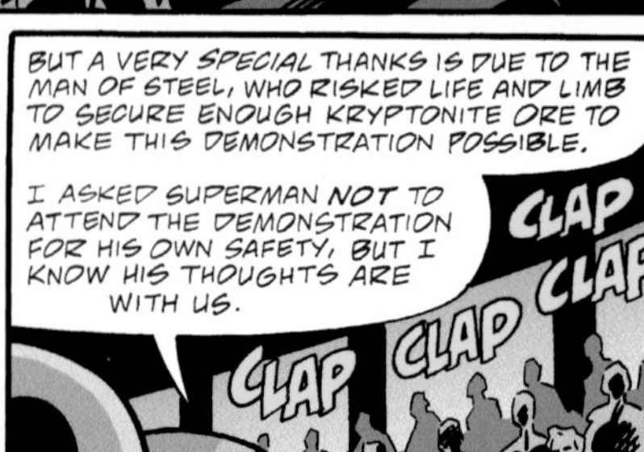

BUT A VERY *SPECIAL* THANKS IS DUE TO THE MAN OF STEEL, WHO RISKED LIFE AND LIMB TO SECURE ENOUGH KRYPTONITE ORE TO MAKE THIS DEMONSTRATION POSSIBLE.

I ASKED SUPERMAN ***NOT*** TO ATTEND THE DEMONSTRATION FOR HIS OWN SAFETY, BUT I KNOW HIS THOUGHTS ARE WITH US.

OF COURSE, PROFESSOR. NOW, ONCE THE CHAIN REACTION SETS IN, THESE TRANSFORMERS WILL SEND THE ENERGY DOWNFIELD TO THE THERMODYNE TERMINALS,

"AND TONIGHT, THE GREAT STATES OF TEXAS, ARIZONA, AND NEW MEXICO WILL SWITCH OVER TO THE LEXCORP POWER GRID AND EVERY LIGHT WILL BURN BRIGHTLY--CLEANLY--ON K-POWER!"
LOS OTROS, NEW MEXICO
LEXCORP TESTING GROUNDS

YOU KNOW, CLARK, YOU WERE AWFULLY QUIET ON THE WAY HERE. IS SOMETHING BOTHERING YOU?
NO. NO, MAYBE I'M A LITTLE AWE-STRUCK ABOUT THE IMPLICATIONS...

WHICH? THE IDEA OF AN ENDLESS SUPPLY OF NONPOLLUTING ENERGY, OR THE FACT THAT LEX LUTHOR MIGHT END UP BEING REGARDED AS A BIGGER HERO THAN SUPERMAN?

MISTER BONHAM. IF YOU WILL?

THRUMMMMMMMMM

BONHAM! WHAT'S HAPPENING?!
I--I DON'T KNOW, SIR! IT'S APPROACHING CRITICAL MASS!

WHAT ARE YOU SAYING?!

THAT WE'RE FACING A MELTDOWN?
WORSE. A DETONATION!

CH-KLANG!

IT'S GOING TO BLOW!
GOOD LORD!

CHUNG!

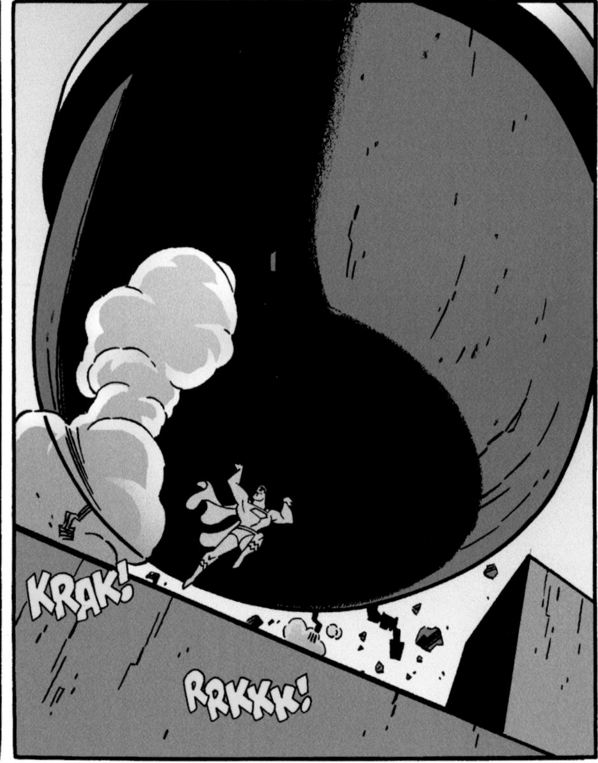
KRAK!
RRKKK!

SHHHH...

KOWWW!

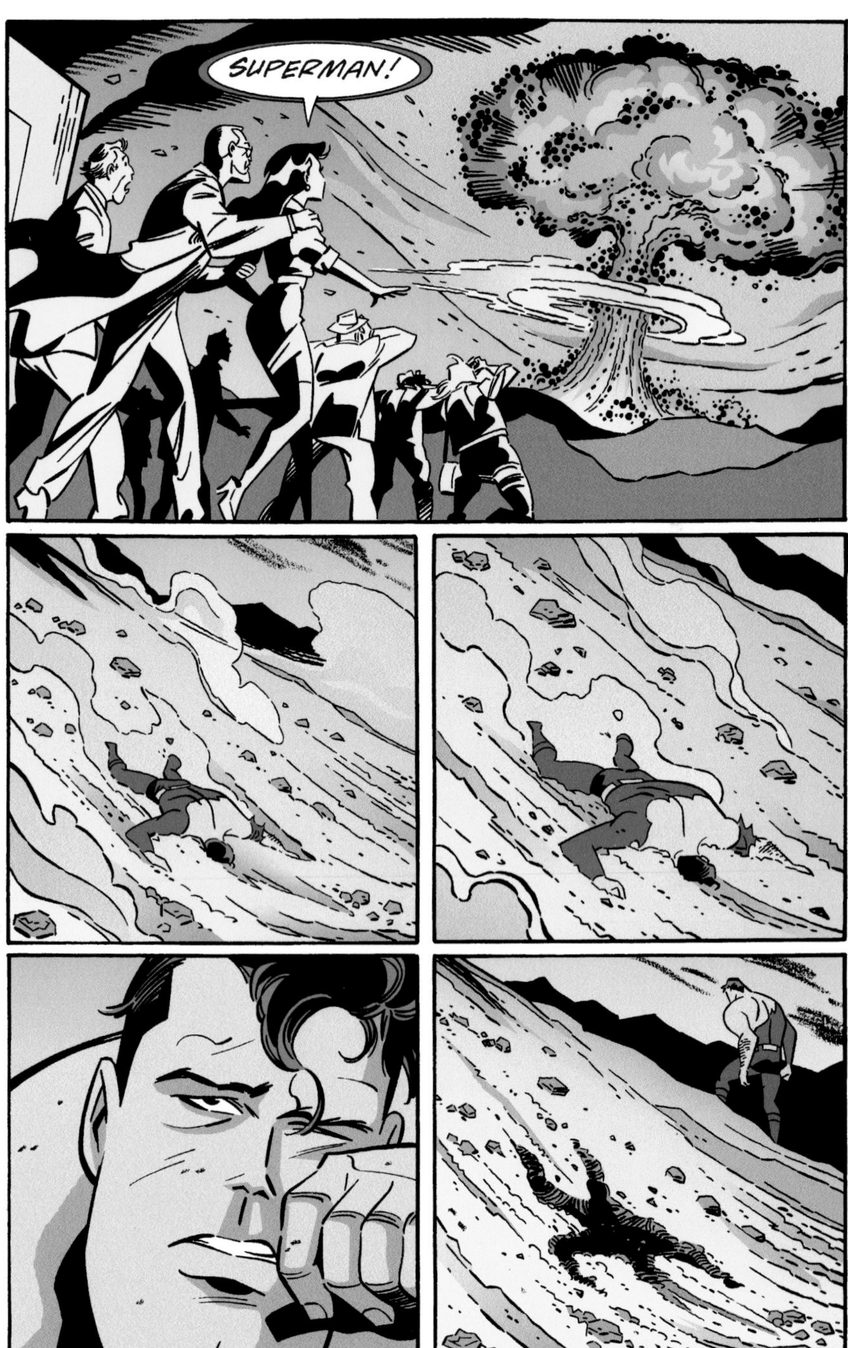
SUPERMAN!

AMAZING! IF I DIDN'T KNOW ANY BETTER I'D SWEAR THE BLAST AND RESIDUE HAVE HAD NO SIGNIFICANT EFFECT ON YOU!
HOW IS YOUR HEADACHE?
IT SEEMS TO HAVE PASSED.

WELL?
I CAN'T BE CERTAIN-- BUT IT APPEARS THAT THERE WERE SOME-- ER--IMPURITIES IN OUR SPECIMEN...

IMPURITIES? I DON'T LIKE IMPURITIES, MISTER BONHAM! I MAKE EVERY EFFORT TO ELIMINATE THEM.

AND THOSE FRAGMENTS...
NOTHING, PROFESSOR. THE MATERIAL HAS REVERTED TO A NONRADIO-ACTIVE STATE. IT IS COMPLETELY INERT.

NEEDS SALT.

IF THIS MEANS WHAT I THINK IT MEANS--

--THE EXPLOSION HAS ALTERED THE ATOMIC WEIGHT OF THE ISOTOPE. IT MIGHT AS WELL BE ORDINARY--UH--PUMICE!
CRNCH!

"THE EFFECTS OF THE KRYPTONITE ARE COMPLETELY NEUTRALIZED, SUPERMAN!

"THIS IS INCREDIBLE! IT APPEARS THERE IS NOW NOTHING IN THE KNOWN UNIVERSE THAT CAN HARM YOU!"

DAILY PLANE
WELL DONE, BOYS AND GIRLS!

NOW, THAT'S WHAT I CALL REPORTING!
DAILY PLANET
PRICE: $1.25
MONDAY, JULY 24, 2001
ELECTRIC DREAMS SHORT-CIRCUITED; LEXCORP'S UTOPIAN POWER GOES UP IN SMOKE

BUT WHY DID WE BURY THE SUPERMAN ANGLE ON PAGE FIVE?
WELL, LOIS... WE STILL DON'T REALLY KNOW MUCH ABOUT IT--
SO THIS KRYPTONITE NO ONE HAS EVER HEARD OF IS JUST AS HARMLESS TO SUPERMAN AS ANY-BODY ELSE! SO WHAT?
IT'S NOT AS BIG AS LUTHOR'S ENERGY SCHEME GOING BUST!

I DON'T AGREE. WHEN IT COMES DOWN TO IT, THE ONLY THING THAT REALLY HAS CHANGED IS SUPERMAN!

LOIS, WHY ARE YOU RAINING ON YOUR OWN PARADE? WHY DON'T YOU FIND OUT WHAT HE WAS DOING THERE IN THE FIRST PLACE? OR WHAT LUTHOR'S PLANS ARE NOW?

PLANET
I WANT YOUR FOLLOW-UPS ON MY DESK--IN THE A.M.!

BY THE WAY, SMALLVILLE, WHAT HAPPENED TO YOU DURING THE EXPLOSION?
KENT! ARE YOU OKAY? WHAT'S THE MATTER?

KKRAASH!
WHAT TH--?!

SUPERMAN?!
I-I DON'T THINK THAT'S SUPERMAN...
TO BE CONTINUED NEXT ISSUE!

LEX LUTHOR
MAN OF METROPOLIS

KRYPTONITE NO MORE!
PART TWO
SUPERMAN CREATED BY...
JERRY SIEGEL & JOE SHUSTER
SUPER-MAN?!
I-I DON'T THINK THAT'S SUPERMAN...
DEAN MOTTER——WRITER
ALUIR AMANCIO—PENCILLER
TERRY AUSTIN——INKER
PHIL FELIX——LETTERER
MARIE SEVERIN—COLORIST
ZYLONOL—— SEPARATIONS
JOEY CAVALIERI——EDITOR
INSPIRED BY DENNIS O'NEIL, CURT SWAN AND MURPHY ANDERSON

KRAK!
EVERY-BODY! TO THE DOOR!
LOOK OUT!

WHO... WHAT... IS THIS?

CRASH!

Unnnhh...

LOOK OUT!

CRUSSH!

THIS THING JUST KEEPS PICKING A FIGHT!

IT'S FIXATED ON ME... GOES WHERE I GO!
THUD!

AAAGH!

SWOOOSH!
GOT TO LEAD HIM AWAY FROM THE CITY!

WHAT? BEHIND ME--SO FAST...

LET'S SEE IF IT KEEPS UP--NOW!
BUR-ROOOM!

WELL, WE'VE EXAMINED YOU HEAD TO TOE. THERE'S NOTHING WRONG THAT WE CAN FIND.

IT APPEARS THAT THE WEAKNESS AND PAIN YOU EXPERIENCED WITH THIS CREATURE WAS TEMPORARY.
IT FELT LIKE--KRYPTONITE WHEN I TOUCHED IT. IS THAT POSSIBLE? DIDN'T THE EXPLOSION RENDER ALL KRYPTONITE INERT?
IT CERTAINLY SEEMS TO BE RELATED.

ANY IDEA WHAT THIS BEING IS?
NOT EXACTLY. BUT IT'S NOT ALIVE. MY THEORY IS THAT IT IS NOT SO MUCH A CREATURE AS A REFLECTION.
A REFLECTION?!

A KIND OF QUANTUM DOPPELGANGER--OF YOU! IT IS DRAWN TO YOU, IT MIMICS YOU, IT ABSORBS YOUR POWERS, IT EXISTS TO OBLITERATE AND REPLACE YOU IN THE PHYSICAL UNIVERSE.
THERE IS A SUBATOMIC PARTICLE CALLED A PHAENTUM THAT BEHAVES IN MUCH THE SAME WAY WHEN CLOSE TO ITS PROGENITOR--
--WHICH IT INEVITABLY DESTROYS.

THIS MAY BE THE BASIS FOR YOUR "COUNTERPART."
WHERE COULD IT HAVE COME FROM? WHO CREATED IT?

YOU.
IST
32 par cm
ME?!

IN A MANNER OF SPEAKING. TAKE A LOOK AT THIS TAPE.
LUTHOR'S FOLLY: K-POWER A BUST!
THE NIGHT THE LIGHTS WENT OUT IN UTOPIA
WHAT IS IT?
I WAS GOING OVER THE LOS OTROS FOOTAGE TRYING TO FIND OUT WHAT WENT WRONG. WE CAUGHT THIS AT THE END OF THE TAPE...

...AND THEN THIS SHOWS UP ON THE NEWS THE NEXT DAY!
I DON'T HAVE TO TELL YOU THE PUBLICITY OVER THE K-POWER FIASCO HAS BEEN DISASTROUS.
MISTER BONHAM, YOU MAY HAVE JUST BOUGHT YOURSELF A REPRIEVE.

NO, SIR...
TAKE THE PROJECT STAFF AND LOOK INTO THIS. LOCATE IT AND FIND OUT EVERYTHING YOU CAN. THIS IS YOUR CHANCE TO TURN CALAMITY INTO FORTUNE.
THANK YOU, MISTER LUTHOR.

AND MISTER BONHAM...
FEW GET A SECOND CHANCE...
YES, SIR.

CLARK! ARE YOU ALL RIGHT? WHERE ON EARTH HAVE YOU BEEN?
IT'S A LONG STORY. BUT I'M AFRAID I'M GOING TO BE AWAY FOR A WHILE.
WHAT--WAIT A MINUTE! WHAT HAPPENED TO YOU AFTER--?

I'VE GOT A LEAD ON THAT CREATURE THAT ATTACKED THE DAILY PLANET. I'M GOING TO FOLLOW IT UP!

ALONE?! I DON'T THINK SO.
I CAN'T TALK FURTHER. I'LL CALL YOU LATER.
CLICK!

HOPEFULLY THIS WON'T TAKE LONG. THIS FAR UNDERGROUND THERE IS VIRTUALLY NO BACK-GROUND RADIATION, SO WE CAN MEASURE TO WHAT DEGREE YOU'RE "CONNECTED" TO THE PHAENTUM-- "CREATURE".
THIS WON'T HURT A BIT.

IT TICKLES!
WAIT A MINUTE--

--THERE'S A MASSIVE DISTURBANCE--

KRASSHH!
IT'S FOUND US!

WAM!
GET BACK!

WUP!
WUP!
WUP!
POW!

SUPERMAN! THOSE BAFFLES-- THEY'RE LEAD!

WHILE-- I STILL-- HAVE THE STRENGTH...
... GOT TO MELT THE LEAD... WITH MY HEAT VISION--
--AND FORM A PROTECTIVE COVERING!
NOW WHAT?
GAAAR!
THOOOOM!

CRASH!
WHAM!
SKAASH!
WOOOM!
CRASH!
SHKOW!

RRRUMBLE!
WE'RE TUNNELING THROUGH THE EARTH...

...INTO A VOLCANIC FISSURE!

WE'RE EMERGING FROM... A VOLCANO! WE'RE SOMEWHERE IN CENTRAL AMERICA!

GREAT KRYPTON! IS IT--IS IT MELTING?

NO!

THE CREATURE'S TRANSFORMED INTO A LAVA-BEING!

CAPTAIN! SLOW ONE QUARTER! WE'RE GOING TO BRING THIS ONE IN.
LEX, DON'T YOU THINK YOU'RE BEING A LITTLE -- HEARTLESS? THE POOR, DEFENSELESS CREATURE DOESN'T STAND A CHANCE --
HE ISN'T DEFENSE-LESS, MY DEAR. HE HAS BEEN A DANGEROUS ADVERSARY FOR A LONG TIME.
I'M SIMPLY SHOWING HIM WHO'S MASTER. BESIDES, I THOUGHT YOU FOUND MY "HEARTLESSNESS" ATTRACTIVE.
YOU ARE TALKING ABOUT THE SHARK, AREN'T YOU?
YOU HAVE A CALL FROM LOS OTROS, MISTER LUTHOR.
PUT IT THROUGH.

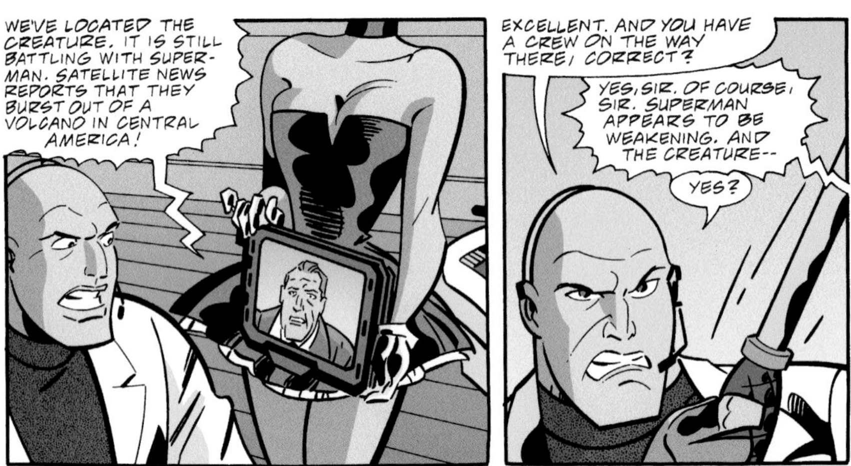

WE'VE LOCATED THE CREATURE. IT IS STILL BATTLING WITH SUPER-MAN. SATELLITE NEWS REPORTS THAT THEY BURST OUT OF A VOLCANO IN CENTRAL AMERICA!
EXCELLENT. AND YOU HAVE A CREW ON THE WAY THERE, CORRECT?
YES, SIR. OF COURSE, SIR. SUPERMAN APPEARS TO BE WEAKENING. AND THE CREATURE--
YES?

IT APPEARS TO HAVE TRANSFORMED SOMEHOW...
PERHAPS IT WILL FINISH ITS WORK BEFORE YOU GET THERE. THEN IT WILL BE A MENACE TO SOCIETY... AND WE WILL BE BLAMED FOR UNLEASHING IT...
I WANT YOU TO LURE SUPERMAN TO THE LOS OTROS TEST SITE.
BUT THE CREATURE--

DON'T WORRY. WHATEVER THAT THING IS, THE HUNTER WON'T REST UNTIL IT HAS FINISHED WITH ITS QUARRY.

NOR WILL I...

SHKOW!
KARAAK!
SPLAAK!
ESSELTE
one

CRASH!
=UNNFF!= I'VE GOT TO LURE THIS THING AWAY FROM THE PEOPLE--

WAIT! WHAT'S THAT I HEAR?
A CHOPPER?

SHHUU
MMM

WOOOOM!

THANKS, BUT IT WON'T BE DOWN FOR LONG! YOU'D BETTER HEAD FOR SAFETY!
WE HAVE A WAY TO STOP IT, SUPERMAN! WE KNOW HOW TO REVERSE THE EFFECTS!

L-LUTHOR? GIVE ME A BREAK...
YOU MUST HEAD TO LOS OTROS! THE THING WILL FOLLOW YOU!

YOU DON'T STAND A CHANCE WITH-OUT OUR HELP! WE'VE SET A TRAP --BUT YOU'LL HAVE TO BE THE BAIT!

GAAAR!

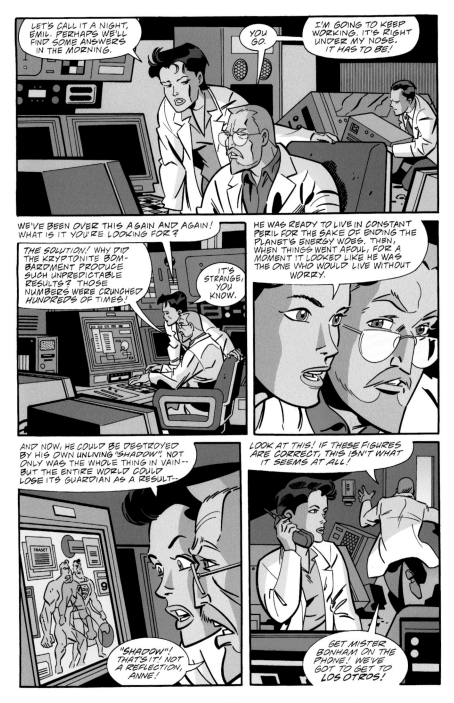

LET'S CALL IT A NIGHT, EMIL. PERHAPS WE'LL FIND SOME ANSWERS IN THE MORNING.
YOU GO.
I'M GOING TO KEEP WORKING. IT'S RIGHT UNDER MY NOSE. IT HAS TO BE!

WE'VE BEEN OVER THIS AGAIN AND AGAIN! WHAT IS IT YOU'RE LOOKING FOR?
THE SOLUTION! WHY DID THE KRYPTONITE BOMBARDMENT PRODUCE SUCH UNPREDICTABLE RESULTS? THOSE NUMBERS WERE CRUNCHED HUNDREDS OF TIMES!
IT'S STRANGE, YOU KNOW.
HE WAS READY TO LIVE IN CONSTANT PERIL FOR THE SAKE OF ENDING THE PLANET'S ENERGY WOES. THEN, WHEN THINGS WENT AFOUL, FOR A MOMENT IT LOOKED LIKE HE WAS THE ONE WHO WOULD LIVE WITHOUT WORRY.

AND NOW, HE COULD BE DESTROYED BY HIS OWN UNLIVING "SHADOW". NOT ONLY WAS THE WHOLE THING IN VAIN-- BUT THE ENTIRE WORLD COULD LOSE ITS GUARDIAN AS A RESULT--
TRASET
9
"SHADOW"! THAT'S IT! NOT A REFLECTION, ANNE!

LOOK AT THIS! IF THESE FIGURES ARE CORRECT, THIS ISN'T WHAT IT SEEMS AT ALL!
GET MISTER BONHAM ON THE PHONE! WE'VE GOT TO GET TO LOS OTROS!

"IT LOOKS LIKE SUPERMAN BOUGHT THE STORY, MR. LUTHOR."
LEXCORP
LOS OTROS
TESTING GRO
NO UNAUTHOR
PERSONNE
DAN
"WHY WOULDN'T HE?

"HE KNOWS WHAT I HAVE TO LOSE IF THAT CREATURE DESTROYS HIM AND IS TURNED LOOSE ON MANKIND. ONLY I CAN SAVE THE DAY THIS TIME, MR. BONHAM.
BAAM!

"IT'S UNFORTUNATE THAT IT WILL INVOLVE HIS 'ACCIDENTAL' DEMISE AS WELL--

FTOOM!
SHAAK!
ZOK!
BOOMP!
"--BUT THEN THAT'S THE PRICE OF SAVING THE WORLD."

IT'S IMPORTANT THAT YOU DEPLOY THE DEVICE WHILE THEY'RE BOTH AT GROUND ZERO.
WHAT'S OUR MARGIN?
NO MARGIN! AS LONG AS THE ENTITY IS IN CONTACT WITH SUPERMAN IT'S SIPHONING THE ENERGY FROM HIM! THE MOMENT IT REACHES FULL CAPACITY IT WILL BE INVULNERABLE!
THE DETONATION MUST OCCUR WHILE THEY'RE BOTH AT 50%!
I HEARD THE COCKPIT TRANSMISSION WITH MY SUPER-HEARING! I DON'T KNOW HOW LEX PLANS TO STRIKE...
...BUT I'VE GOT TO SEE THIS THROUGH! ESPECIALLY IF IT MIGHT ENDANGER OTHERS!
ANYTIME, LUTHOR--
A BOMB! I SHOULD HAVE KNOWN...
IF I'M GOING, AT LEAST I CAN RID MY WORLD OF YOU...

WE'LL GO -- UNHH -- TOGETHER!
KA
BOOOOOOM

THE MORNING AFTER...
THE RADIATION LEVELS ARE FALLING, PROFESSOR. IT LOOKS SAFE TO APPROACH.

EVERYTHING HAS BEEN COMPLETELY VAPORIZED. THE KRYPTONITE, THE STRUCTURES-- LUTHOR MAY HAVE USED A LOW RAD DEVICE, BUT IT SURE PACKED A WALLOP!
UP AHEAD!

OH, NO!

KRUSH!

SUPERMAN!

I'M WAITING, MISTER BONHAM.
LEXCORP

MY PEOPLE HAVE COLLATED THE FINAL DATA--UH, SIR.
THE REACTOR NEVER REALLY AFFECTED THE KRYPTONITE AT ALL. AMAZING, huh? THE INITIAL READINGS WERE MORE LIKE--WELL--SHADOWS OF READINGS. THE ISOTOPE'S ATOMIC WEIGHT WAS UNCHANGED AFTER ALL.
AND SUPERMAN?
THE CHAIN REACTION ACTUALLY ALTERED HIS MOLECULAR STRUCTURE--NOT THE KRYPTONITE'S.

IT ALSO CREATED THE QUANTUM ENTITY--A SORT OF ANTI-MATTER REFLECTION OF--WELL, ANYWAY--ONCE THE ATOMIC EXPLOSION COLLAPSED ITS FIELD COHESION THE ENTITY WAS NO LONGER VIABLE AND SUPERMAN REVERTED TO HIS PRIOR--Um--STATE OF--

ENOUGH...

THE PROCESS WAS SOMEWHAT OF A FLUKE, BUT THAT DOESN'T MEAN THAT OUR ORIGINAL THEORY WAS VERY FAR OFF! WITH A LITTLE MORE RESEARCH, WE COULD--

I THINK NOT.

MERCY, BE GOOD ENOUGH TO DRIVE MISTER BONHAM TO HIS NEXT APPOINTMENT.
FINIS

LEX

LEX LUTHOR, MAN OF METROPOLIS

--SO WE'RE LOOKING AT SEVERE THUNDERSTORMS HEADING OUR WAY TONIGHT. BATTEN DOWN THE HATCHES, METROPOLIS; THINGS ARE GOING TO GET PRETTY WILD.
MARLA?
THANKS, CHUCK. SPEAKING OF "PRETTY WILD," WE HAVE BREAKING NEWS THAT A DECISION HAS BEEN MADE IN THE SO-CALLED "LIVEWIRE CUSTODY BATTLE" BETWEEN LEX LUTHOR AND S.T.A.R. LABS.
HERE'S ANGELA CHEN WITH THE LATEST ON THIS MOST ELECTRIFYING CASE...
MARLA, I'M STANDING OUTSIDE S.T.A.R. LABS, WHICH FOR SEVERAL MONTHS NOW HAS BEEN HOME TO LESLIE WILLIS, THE FORMER K-LEX SHOCK JOCK KNOWN BETTER TODAY AS THE ELECTRICALLY CHARGED SUPERBEING CALLED LIVEWIRE.
"ALTHOUGH ORIGINALLY A CRIMINAL MENACE, VIEWERS WILL RECALL HOW MONTHS AGO LIVEWIRE SACRIFICED HERSELF TO SAVE THE WORLD FROM DESTRUCTION AT THE HANDS OF BRAINIAC.
"SINCE THEN, SHE'S REMAINED IN A COMA, POWERLESS AND IMMOBILE DESPITE S.T.A.R. LABS' EFFORTS TO REVIVE HER.
"THIS FAILURE HAS BROUGHT ON A STORM OF CONTROVERSY--
"--STEMMING FROM A LAWSUIT INITIATED BY LEX LUTHOR AGAINST S.T.A.R. LABS, SEEKING CUSTODY AND CARE OF LIVEWIRE."
AS YOU ALL KNOW, I'VE CONTINUALLY TAKEN MEDICAL AND LEGAL RESPONSIBILITY FOR MY FORMER EMPLOYEE SINCE THE UNFORTUNATE ACCIDENT THAT CHANGED HER.
FREE LESLIE

CAN HE
MS. WILLIS SACRIFICED HERSELF TO SAVE US, AND HOW HAVE WE SHOWN OUR GRATITUDE? BY LOCKING HER UP IN S.T.A.R. LABS TO BE POKED AND PRODDED LIKE ONE OF THEIR GUINEA PIGS! WELL, I SAY ENOUGH!
"FOR HIS PART, S.T.A.R. LABS' DIRECTOR EMIL HAMILTON HAD THIS TO SAY--"
I REFUSE TO PARTICIPATE IN THE MEDIA CIRCUS THAT MR. LUTHOR IS RINGLEADING.
HOWEVER, I CAN ASSURE YOU WE ARE DOING EVERYTHING WE CAN FOR MS. WILLIS.
"BUT PUBLIC SENTIMENT DOESN'T SEEM TO AGREE WITH PROFESSOR HAMILTON."
S.T.A.R. HASN'T DONE SQUAT FOR LIVEWIRE!
I BET LEX COULD CURE HER IN NO TIME, I MEAN, HE'S A GENIUS!
"AND WHAT ABOUT SUPERMAN? SOME STILL CONSIDER HIM RESPONSIBLE FOR THE ACCIDENT THAT TRANSFORMED LESLIE WILLIS INTO LIVEWIRE.
"WE ASKED THE MAN OF STEEL'S OPINION ON THE CASE, BUT ALL HE HAD TO SAY WAS--"
NO COMMENT.
WHATEVER THE ARGUMENTS, JUDGE BURNLEY RULED TODAY IN FAVOR OF LEX LUTHOR--
--WHO IS HERE PREPARING TO TAKE LIVEWIRE TO HIS OWN MEDICAL FACILITIES--

POWER PLAY PART ONE

EVAN DORKIN & SARAH DYER, WRITERS
ALUIR AMANCIO, PENCILS TERRY AUSTIN, INKS
PHIL FELIX, LETTERS MARIE SEVERIN, COLORS
ZYLONOL, SEPARATOR JOEY CAVALIERI, EDITOR

--AND I PROMISE TO DEVOTE ALL OF LEXCORP'S RESOURCES TO RESTORING MS. WILLIS. IT'S THE LEAST I CAN DO TO REPAY HER FOR HER SACRIFICE.
NOW, IF YOU WILL ALL EXCUSE ME, I'LL BE SEEING MS. WILLIS HOME.

WHY, IF IT ISN'T SUPERMAN! COME TO WISH LESLIE BON VOYAGE? OR ARE THINGS SO BAD YOU'RE FORCED TO WORK AS PART-TIME SECURITY FOR OLD EMIL HERE?

I'M SURE THEY COULD USE YOU, WITH THE ATROCIOUS RECORD OF ACCIDENTS AND BREAK-INS THEY HAVE--
THAT'S ENOUGH, LUTHOR.
JUST REMEMBER... I'LL BE KEEPING AN EYE ON YOU.
OH, MY. HOWEVER WILL I SLEEP AT NIGHT? DON'T WORRY ABOUT MS. WILLIS, SUPERMAN. HER SAFETY IS OF THE UTMOST IMPORTANCE TO ME.

WELL, I GUESS ALL WE CAN DO NOW IS HOPE THAT SOMEHOW LUTHOR REALLY DOES HAVE LESLIE'S BEST INTERESTS IN MIND.
LEX LUTHOR ONLY HAS ONE INTEREST IN THIS WORLD. AND THAT'S LEX LUTHOR.

Hmmm. SOMETHING ABOUT THAT GURNEY THEY HAD LIVEWIRE IN IS BOTHERING ME... AND OF COURSE, LUTHOR'S LIMO IS SHIELDED FROM MY X-RAY VISION...

"...RIGHT NOW I'D GIVE ANYTHING TO SEE WHAT'S GOING ON IN THERE."
SO, LUTHOR... I TRUST THAT EVERYTHING WENT SMOOTHLY?
BUT OF COURSE, MY GOOD MAN. YOU CAN SEE I HAVE THE GIRL.
GOOD. NOW LET'S JUST SEE HOW BADLY YOUR CHARGE HAS BEEN DAMAGED.
FOR THAT, WE WILL NEED TO AWAKEN OUR LITTLE SLEEPING BEAUTY.

BRAIN FUNCTIONS NORMALIZING--SHE'S AWAKE! FINAL READINGS INDICATE SHE'S DEPOWERED BUT INTACT--

PERFECT! YOUR DEVICE ACCOMPLISHED IN SECONDS WHAT S.T.A.R. COULDN'T DO IN MONTHS! I'M IMPRESSED--

BUT OF COURSE.

ZMMMMMMMMMMMMM

OH, MAN... WHO PUT COTTON IN MY MOUTH... AND BRAIN?

WELCOME BACK, LESLIE. YOU'VE BEEN VERY ILL--NOTHING MUCH, A MERE COMA--BUT WE'VE PUT YOU TO RIGHTS.

WELL THAT'S REAL SWELL AND ALL, LEX, BUT WHO ARE THESE PEOPLE? AND WHY AM I STRAPPED DOWN LIKE FRANKENSTEIN'S SCIENCE PROJECT?

IT WAS MERELY FOR YOUR OWN PROTECTION.

SEE? YOU'RE FREE AS A BIRD NOW.
THANKS. SAY, LEXXY, WOULD YOU MIND DROPPING ME OFF AT--

SORRY, LESLIE, BUT I'VE ARRANGED FOR YOU TO GO ON A LITTLE OUT-OF-TOWN BUSINESS TRIP WITH MY ASSOCIATE HERE.
Uhh, NOT TO SOUND UNAPPRECIATIVE, BUT I'M NOT THAT KIND OF GIRL--

PLEASE--THIS IS STRICTLY BUSINESS. AFTER ALL I'VE DONE FOR YOU I THINK YOU CAN DO ME THIS ONE SMALL FAVOR IN RETURN.
HEY! HOW'S ABOUT I SUPPLY LEXCORP'S POWER FREE FOR A MONTH, INSTEAD? Y'KNOW, STEAL IT FROM THE CITY GRID--
INSOLENT FEMALE! SUCH IMPUDENCE!

WHAT? HEY, JUST WHO IS THIS CREEP, ANYWAY? OWW! LEX, WHAT GIVES?!
DON'T LOOK SO SHOCKED, MY DEAR.
MY BENEVOLENCE TOWARDS YOU HAS BEEN NOTHING MORE THAN A LONG-TERM BUSINESS INVESTMENT--ONE THAT IS ABOUT TO PAY OFF HANDSOMELY, WHETHER YOU LIKE IT OR NOT!

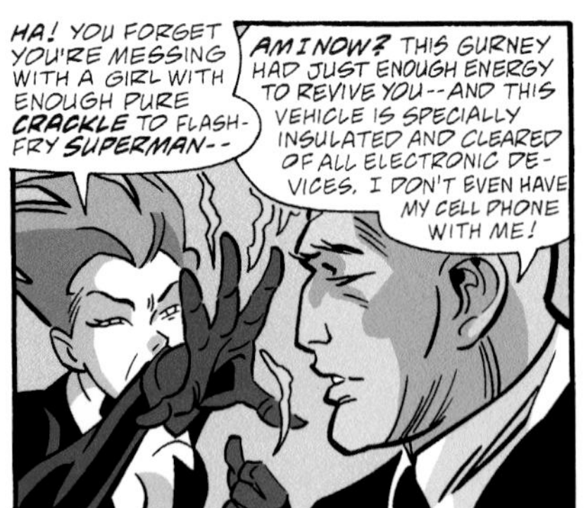
HA! YOU FORGET YOU'RE MESSING WITH A GIRL WITH ENOUGH PURE CRACKLE TO FLASH-FRY SUPERMAN--
AM I NOW? THIS GURNEY HAD JUST ENOUGH ENERGY TO REVIVE YOU--AND THIS VEHICLE IS SPECIALLY INSULATED AND CLEARED OF ALL ELECTRONIC DE-VICES. I DON'T EVEN HAVE MY CELL PHONE WITH ME!

SO YOU'RE LITERALLY POWERLESS TO STOP ME FROM CONCLUDING THIS BUSINESS ARRANGEMENT.
MERCY! I WANT TO BE IN MY OFFICE IN TEN MINUTES, AND NOT A SECOND LATER!

"RUN EVERY RED LIGHT IN ME-TROPOLIS IF YOU HAVE TO!"
THIS IS JUST GREAT! OUT OF THE COMA AND INTO THE FRY-ING PAN! AND I THOUGHT LEX LIKED ME!
HEY NOW, IS THAT WHAT I THINK IT IS? I CAN'T BELIEVE LEX'S TECH GEEKS MISSED THAT! NOW IF I COULD JUST GET A CHANCE TO CAPITALIZE ON THIS...
IF ONLY THERE WAS SOME WAY TO GET MY HANDS ON SOME JOLT JUICE-- I'D LIGHT UP THAT CHROMEDOME LIKE A THOUSAND-WATT BULB!

M-MS. GRAVES! THAT TRAIN-- YOU'RE GONNA--
RELAX, TOMPKINS.

THAT'S WHY CARS HAVE BRAKES!
SKREEEE!

WHAT THE-- STOP HER!
'SCUSE ME FOLKS, BUT I GOT AN ESCAPE PLAN TO HATCH HERE!

HEY!
SHE'S GOING FOR THE CIGARETTE LIGHTER! STOP HER BEFORE--
TOO LATE, SISTER--

TDZAAAAK!
--'CAUSE THIS WIRE'S ALIVE!
HAHAHAH! SWEEEET! WHAT A JUICY CAR BATTERY!

Aw, NOT AGAIN! BLASTING THE CAR MUST HAVE USED UP ALL MY ZAPPAGE!
SHE'S HELPLESS! TAKE HER!
PFFZT!

ALL RIGHT, SPARKPLUG--TIME TO PUT YOUR LIGHTS OUT!
HEEE-YAA!

OH, YEAH? EAT HUBCAP, TOUGH GIRL!
WOOUF!
HOW'S THAT FOR HELPLESS?

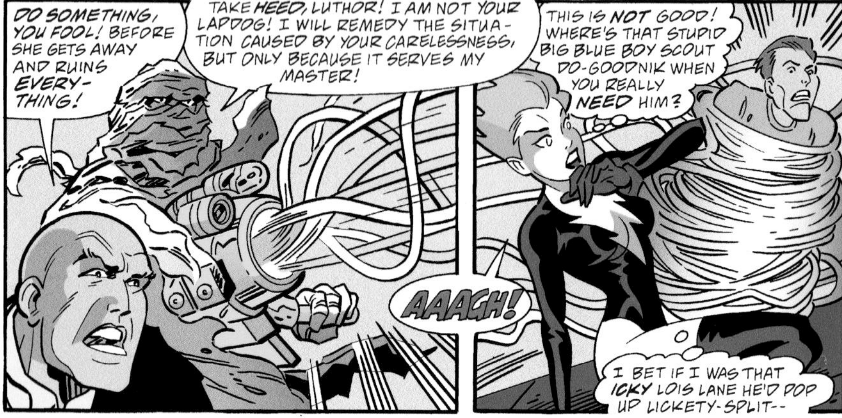

DO SOMETHING, YOU FOOL! BEFORE SHE GETS AWAY AND RUINS EVERY-THING!
TAKE HEED, LUTHOR! I AM NOT YOUR LAPDOG! I WILL REMEDY THE SITUA-TION CAUSED BY YOUR CARELESSNESS, BUT ONLY BECAUSE IT SERVES MY MASTER!
THIS IS NOT GOOD! WHERE'S THAT STUPID BIG BLUE BOY SCOUT DO-GOODNIK WHEN YOU REALLY NEED HIM?
AAAGH!
I BET IF I WAS THAT ICKY LOIS LANE HE'D POP UP LICKETY-SPLIT--

WAAAGHH!
AFTER-NOON, LESLIE. I SEE YOU'RE UP AND ABOUT!
NOW WAITAMINNIT, YOU, I DIDN'T DO NOTHIN'--
LESLIE--

--WELL I DID BLOW UP LUTHOR'S CAR AND HIT HIS CHAUFFEUR BUT I HAD TO, REALLY...
LESLIE, I'M--
WOULD YOU SHUT UP AND LISTEN TO ME, YOU BIG BLUE OX? I'M TRYING TO TELL YOU WHAT HAPPENED--

YEEARGH!
FZZZAT!
SUPERMAN!

ARE YOU INSANE? USING AN ENERGY WEAPON?! YOU COULD HAVE EM-POWERED THE GIRL!
BE STILL, LUTHOR! THIS IS NO BOARDROOM MEETING! THIS IS MORTAL COMBAT-- AND HERE I AM MASTER!

I WAS PREPARED FOR SUPERMAN'S INTERFERENCE. AFTER ALL, ONE MUST ALWAYS EXPECT EARTH'S SHEPHERD TO TEND TO HIS WEAK LITTLE SHEEP.
THAT PERFECTLY PLACED SHOT FROM MY ENERGY WEAPON WAS MEANT TO MERELY SOFTEN UP THE KRYPTONIAN.
THIS, HOWEVER, IS WHAT I WILL SLAY HIM WITH.

BEAUTIFUL, IS IT NOT? IT FIRES A BARRAGE OF EXPLOSIVE KRYPTONITE SHELLS--
--THE IMPACT OF WHICH SHALL SURELY BRING CERTAIN DEATH TO SOMEONE WITH YOUR, SHALL WE SAY, "UNHEALTHY" REACTION TO HIS NATIVE SOIL. GOODBYE, SUPERMAN.
FSSSSH
K-KLIK!
WHAT? A MISFIRE? BUT-- THAT'S IMPOSSIBLE!

HARDLY. WHILE YOU WERE RANTING ABOUT YOUR GREAT POPGUN, I SIMPLY USED MY HEAT VISION TO FUSE THE BARREL CLOSED. SORRY ABOUT THAT, MISTER--
--OR SHOULD I SAY, KANTO?
KA-WHAM!
FOOMF!

FOOSH!
SO, YOUR MUCH VAUNTED X-RAY VISION FINALLY REVEALED MY IDENTITY TO YOU--BUT NO MATTER!
THE ELEMENT OF SURPRISE MAY BE GONE, BUT THE CERTAINTY OF YOUR DEMISE IS STILL AT HAND!
I DIDN'T NEED MY X-RAY VISION, KANTO--
--YOUR ARSENAL HAS "MADE IN APOKOLIPS" WRITTEN ALL OVER IT. JUST LIKE LIVE-WIRE'S SOUPED-UP GURNEY, WHICH I SHOULD HAVE RECOGNIZED EARLIER.
SHPLUDSH!
DO NOT MOCK THE SUPERIOR TECHNOLOGY OF APOKOLIPS!
COUNTLESS WORLDS HAVE FALLEN PREY TO IT, AS SHALL YOU!

WELL, SINCE YOU GUYS OBVIOUSLY KNOW EACH OTHER, I'LL JUST LEAVE YOU TWO TO ENJOY YOUR FIGHT!
TA-TA!

I DON'T THINK SO--

YOU'VE ONLY SEEN A MERE FRACTION OF MY ARSENAL!

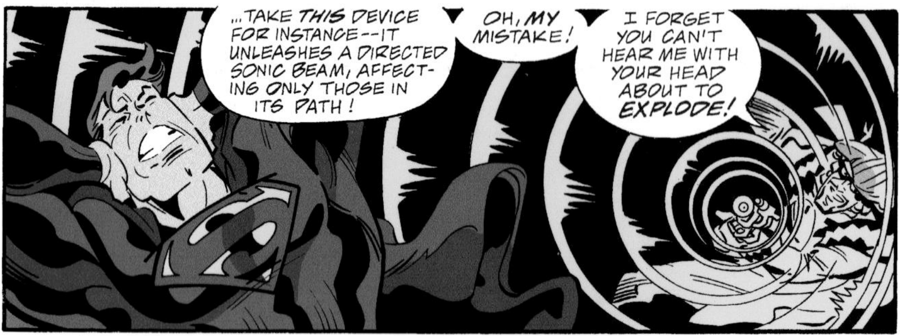
...TAKE THIS DEVICE FOR INSTANCE--IT UNLEASHES A DIRECTED SONIC BEAM, AFFECTING ONLY THOSE IN ITS PATH!
OH, MY MISTAKE!
I FORGET YOU CAN'T HEAR ME WITH YOUR HEAD ABOUT TO EXPLODE!

SORRY KANTO-- WERE YOU SAYING SOMETHING?

HEY! LIVEWIRE'S AWAKE!
BUT SHE'S CRAZIER THAN EVER!
HELLO?! PEOPLE! REMEMBER ME? LIVEWIRE? WORLD SAVIOR AND ALL THAT?! OOF!
I COULD USE A LITTLE HELP HERE, Y'KNOW?! I'M GETTING KINDA BEAT UP IF YOU HADN'T NOTICED!
OW!
ALL RIGHT, FOLKS! EVERY-THING'S UNDER CONTROL!

UNFORTUNATELY, SUPERMAN'S MED-DLING HAS CAUSED MS. WILLIS TO SUFFER A PSYCHOTIC SETBACK!
POOR LEX! AFTER ALL HE'S TRIED TO DO FOR HER!
YOU JERKS DON'T BELIEVE THIS LYING CUEBALL, DO YOU? WELL, FINE! NEXT TIME YOU NEED THE WORLD SAVED, DON'T CALL ME!
HOLD HER STILL, BOSS! I'LL PUT HER OUT QUICK--

--UH, FOR HER OWN GOOD, OF COURSE!
HA! NICE GOING, EMMA PEEL!
KRAK!
OOOF!

HAHAHA! "EMMA PEEL!" SOME-TIMES I CRACK ME UP!

SORRY ABOUT THAT, BOSS...
WELL, DON'T JUST STAND THERE! GET HER!

THIS IS ALMOST TOO EASY--I MUST SAY, I EXPECTED A LITTLE MORE FROM YOU, SUPER--
KZZAK!

--MAAAAAAANNN!
WHOOSHH!

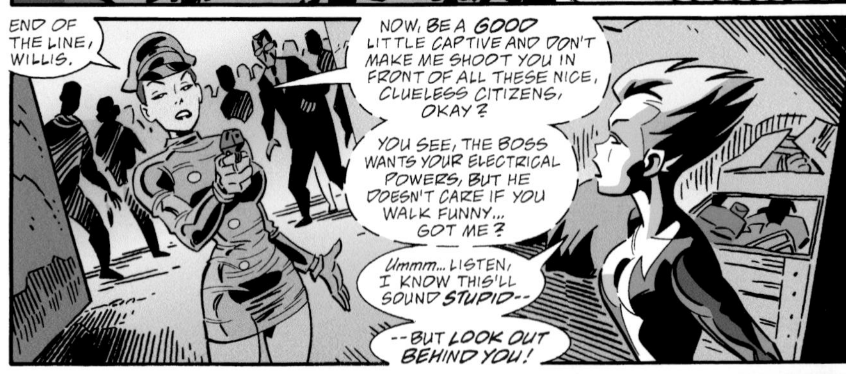
END OF THE LINE, WILLIS.
NOW, BE A GOOD LITTLE CAPTIVE AND DON'T MAKE ME SHOOT YOU IN FRONT OF ALL THESE NICE, CLUELESS CITIZENS, OKAY?
YOU SEE, THE BOSS WANTS YOUR ELECTRICAL POWERS, BUT HE DOESN'T CARE IF YOU WALK FUNNY... GOT ME?
Ummm... LISTEN, I KNOW THIS'LL SOUND STUPID--
--BUT LOOK OUT BEHIND YOU!

DON'T BE A SAP! THAT GUFF ONLY WORKS IN BAD MOVIES!
WELL, OKAY--

YEEEARGH!
UNGH!
--IF YOU SAY SO!
B-THWAM!

LESLIE--ARE YOU ALL RIGHT?
I AM NOW. NICE SHOT WITH THE BIGMOUTH THERE, BY THE WAY!

I'M AFRAID I'LL HAVE TO PUT AN END TO THIS CELEBRATION-- AS WELL AS THIS PATHETIC CREATURE --UNLESS YOU HAND THE GIRL OVER, SUPERMAN!

TAKING A HOSTAGE, KANTO?
ISN'T THAT A LITTLE BENEATH THE SO-CALLED MASTER ASSASSIN OF APOKOLIPS?
MAYBE SO.
BUT YOU KNOW WHO I SERVE, AND HE IS NOT ONE TO BE DISAP-POINTED.

IS THAT SO?
K-CHOOM!

WHAT THE--?
KRAKK!

AAAAAHHH!
DON'T WORRY, MISS. I'VE GOT YOU!

HOW DREARILY COMMENDABLE. BUT I'M AFRAID YOUR POINTLESS CHIVALRY HAS LET YOUR GUARD DROP--ALLOWING ME TO END THIS DUEL HERE AND NOW!

UNGH! THESE DISCS-- I CAN'T GET THEM LOOSE!

THOSE "DISCS," AS YOU SO QUAINTLY CALL THEM, ARE INCENDIARY "SLAYMORES"--EACH CONTAINING ENERGY FROM THE HEART OF APOKOLIPS ITSELF!
WICKED DESAAD DESIGNED THEM SO THAT A SINGLE SLAYMORE WOULD TOPPLE A WARRIOR GOD OF NEW GENESIS! IMAGINE WHAT SEVERAL WILL DO!
HO! I'M IMPRESSED YOU MANAGED TO WRENCH EVEN ONE OF THEM OFF, SUPERMAN!

KWATHOOOM!
BUT YOU'LL NEVER GET THEM ALL OFF BEFORE THEY DETONATE AND YOU ERUPT IN FLAMING DEATH LIKE KRYPTON ITSELF!

WAIT--WHAT ARE YOU DOING?! STOP!
NO! NO! YOU FOOL! THE SLAYMORES ARE SET TO GO OFF ANY SECOND NOW!
I KNOW.
TIK TIK TIK TIK TIK

FA-BA-BAA-THOOOM!

IT'S OVER, KANTO. YOU'VE LOST.
NO... IT CAN'T BE! I HAD PLANNED! I WAS PREPARED!
MAYBE THAT'S YOUR PROBLEM, KANTO. TOO MANY GADGETS AND NOT ENOUGH GUTS!
I RATHER THINK NOT, KRYPTONIAN. YOU MAY HAVE WON THE BATTLE--
PING PING PINNG

--BUT THE WAR'S ONLY JUST BEGUN!
BOOM!
A BOOM TUBE! LESLIE, GET BACK!

KANTO! JUST WHAT DO YOU THINK YOU'RE DOING?! OUR DEAL WAS TO BE SETTLED HERE IN METROPOLIS--THIS ISN'T PART OF OUR AGREEMENT!

NEITHER WAS YOUR ALLOWING THE GIRL TO ESCAPE--

--BRINGING ON THE INTERFERENCE OF THE KRYPTONIAN. NO, LUTHOR, THE SITUATION HAS CHANGED--
--AND A GOOD SOLDIER IS ALWAYS READY TO ADAPT.

AND I, FOR ONE, AM A GREAT SOLDIER, SERVING AN EVEN GREATER CAUSE.
BOOM!

OH, MAN...WHO DECORATED THIS JOINT? THE BLACK PLAGUE?
I SURE DO HOPE I'M STILL IN A COMA HALLUCINATING ALL THIS!
UNFORTUNATELY, THIS IS ALL TOO REAL--
YOU SHOULD BE HONORED TO EVEN SET FOOT ON MAGNIFICENT APOKOLIPS, MY DEAR GIRL. BECAUSE THIS IS WHERE YOU SHALL SOON FIND YOUR GREAT DESTINY--AND WHERE SUPERMAN WILL AT LONG LAST MEET HIS GLORIOUS END!
PHHT! YEAH, RIGHT! YOU AND WHAT ARMY, FAUNTLEROY?
WELL, IF YOU MUST KNOW...

THIS ARMY!
Umm... THIS IS NO BIG DEAL. I MEAN, YOU CAN TAKE THESE CREEPS, RIGHT, SUPERMAN? RIGHT?
SUPERMAN?!

TO BE CONTINUED!

LEX LUTHOR, MAN OF METROPOLIS

POWER PLAY!
PART TWO
YOU MUST ADMIT, IT IS RATHER IMPRESSIVE.
SUPERMAN CREATED BY JERRY SIEGEL & JOE SHUSTER
EVAN DORKIN & SARAH DYER WRITERS
ALUIR AMANCIO PENCILLER
WAYNE FAUCHER INKER
TERRY AUSTIN INKER, PG. 22
PHIL FELIX LETTERER
MARIE SEVERIN COLORIST
ZYLONOL SEPARATOR
JOEY CAVALIERI EDITOR

THE FINEST SHOCK TROOPS APOKOLIPS HAS TO OFFER RAIN DOWN UPON HIM, YET STILL THE KRYPTONIAN PERSEVERES! INDEED, HE RETAINS THE UPPER HAND!
EXCUSE ME, KANTO, BUT THE ONLY RESPECT SUPER-MAN SHOULD BE GIVEN IS HIS LAST RESPECTS!
MUST I REMIND YOU THAT AS LONG AS HE BREATHES HE'S A THREAT TO THE BUSINESS ARRANGE-MENT I'VE MADE WITH YOUR LEADER?
HOLD THY TONGUE, LUTHOR! IT WAS YOUR INCOMPETENCE THAT BROUGHT SUPERMAN TO APOKOLIPS! MY LORD DARKSEID ONLY WANTED THE GIRL!
YEAH, WELL, I DUNNO WHY YOU GOONS BROUGHT ME HERE, BUT IF I GET MY HANDS ON SOME ENERGY, I'M GONNA FRENCH-FRY ALL YOUR BUTTS! THAT GOES DOUBLE FOR YOU, LEX, SELLIN' ME OUT TO THESE--OWWW!
QUIET, YOU SASSY TALKING ANIMAL!
MY DEAR LIVEWIRE... YOUR DOR-MANT ENERGY POWERS CAN-NOT SAVE YOU ANY MORE THAN SUPER-MAN CAN!
NO ONE CAN WITHSTAND OUR ENDLESS RESOURCES, NO MATTER WHAT THEIR STRENGTH!
IF A WARRIOR OF APOKOLIPS FALLS, A HUNDRED SHALL TAKE HIS PLACE! IF A HUNDRED FALL, A THOUSAND SHALL RISE! AND ULTIMATELY THERE IS DARKSEID HIM-SELF, HE WHO IS THE END TO ALL RESISTANCE!

TO SULLY HIS HANDS! SEE? EVEN NOW, SUPERMAN'S DEFEAT IS ASSURED--
ZKRAK!
HEE HEE HEEE!
--AT THE HANDS OF MY FEMALE FURIES!
SEE HOW WELL GRANNY'S GIRLS ARE TRAINED! LASHINA'S WHIP HAS FOUND ITS MARK--AND NOW MAD HARRIET AND STOMPA WILL FINISH THAT MISERABLE OX OFF!
LOOK, GIRLS--THE POOR THING'S TRYING TO PROPOSE!
HAW HAW! INSTEAD OF WEDDED BLISS, HE'S GETTIN' WEDDED BLISTERS!
HEE HEE HEEE!
NO--YOU CAN'T--!
HEE HEE-AAAGH!
YEAAARGH!
BZRAAK!
WELL, THAT WAS CERTAINLY A FINE DISPLAY OF APOKOLIPTIAN RESOURCEFULNESS...
GRANNY, DARKSEID WANTS THE WHELP ALIVE, NOT TAUNTING US WITH HER CHILDISH BRAYING.
YEAH, THAT'S IT, BLUE! SHOW 'EM HOW WE DO THINGS BACK IN METROPOLIS!

ENERGY LANCE, BUT WE CAN'T HAVE YOU POWERED UP AND CAUSING US TROUBLE! SO A SIMPLE BASHED BRAIN IS THE REWARD FOR YOUR BIG MOUTH!
UNNGH!
YOU'RE QUITE ACCOMPLISHED AT RENDERING HELP-LESS GIRLS UN-CONSCIOUS--
--BUT IF YOU HAVEN'T NOTICED, SUPERMAN IS STANDING THERE UNOPPOSED!
AS ALWAYS, LUTHOR, YOU SPEAK TOO RASHLY, AND TOO SOON.
WHAT THE--?
RARRGH!
IT IS TIME THIS SAD SPECTACLE WAS ENDED! AND THUS IS IT TIME FOR THE SON OF DARKSEID--KALIBAK THE CRUEL HIMSELF--TO ENTER THE FRAY!
PREPARE YOUR-SELF, KRYPTONIAN! FOR YOUR END IS AT HAND!
I WAS... WONDERING HOW LONG YOU'D LET YOUR PEONS TAKE A BEATING BEFORE YOU SHOWED YOUR HAND, KALIBAK...
HA! JEALOUS, ARE WE, OF THE STRENGTH OF APOKOLIPS? I CAN UNDERSTAND SUCH BITTER-NESS!

YOU FIGHT ALONE, WITHOUT FRIEND OR ALLY-- WHILE WE ARE MANY, UNITED IN THE ULTIMATE CAUSE!
WHUD!
DEATH AND DEFEAT FOR ALL WHO OPPOSE THE MASTER!
DEATH AND DEFEAT!
THPOW!
I'D DEBATE YOUR DERANGED PHILOSOPHY WITH YOU, KALIBAK--BUT I REALIZE THIS IS THE ONLY ARGUMENT YOUR KIND UNDERSTANDS!
HA!
WAK!
STRONG WORDS FROM ONE WHOSE STRENGTH IS WANING! YOU'VE FOUGHT WELL, SUPERMAN, BUT THE BATTLE HAS TAKEN ITS TOLL!
NOW LET ME SHOW YOU THE FOLLY OF DEFYING MY WORLD--
--BY BURYING YOU DEEP WITHIN THE BOWELS OF APOKOLIPS ITSELF!
KROOOOM!

GOOD LORD! WHAT'S HAPPENING?!
IT IS AN OLD PLOY OF KALIBAK'S--
YES! HE'S TAKEN SUPERMAN BELOW, INTO THE ENERGY PITS THAT POWER ALL OF APOKOLIPS--
"--AND THERE THAT EARTH-LOVING MEATLOAF WILL BE BURNT TO A GREASY CINDER!"
IT'S KALIBAK! WITH ANOTHER VICTIM FOR THE PITS!!
KER-KRUNNCH!
IT IS ENDED! ADMIT DEFEAT, SUPERMAN! LET ALL HEAR THAT KALIBAK IS YOUR BETTER!
NEVER.
AAARGH! MY EYES!!

N-NO, MILORD! PLEASE, I-I'VE DONE NOTHING--!
SILENCE! YOUR MASTER HAS NEED OF YOU! OR WOULD YOU PREFER TO LET THE ENEMY GAIN THE ADVANTAGE WHILE MY SIGHT IS DIMMED?!
NO! NOT THE PIT! I'LL BE INCINERATED! AIIEEE--!
YOU MISERABLE FIEND! HOW COULD YOU?
THAT ONE IS NOTHING TO A HIGH-BORN OF APOKOLIPS! HE IS BUT A TOOL TO BE USED AND DISCARDED--
--A MEANS TO AN END--
--YOUR END!
THAT'S RIGHT, SUPERMAN, SAVE HIM! THAT'S WHAT YOU DO, ISN'T IT?! SAVE THE WEAK, THE USELESS--
--EVEN AT THE EXPENSE OF YOUR OWN LIFE!
AARRGH!
FSHOOOM!
INCREDIBLE. EVEN AFTER THE FURNACE'S SEARING TOUCH, SUPERMAN STILL LIVES!
BUT THAT IS EASILY REMEDIED--
NO, KALIBAK. STAY YOUR VICIOUS HAND.
THE KILLING BLOW WILL BE DELIVERED, BUT ONLY WHEN I DESIRE IT. FOR NOW, LET SUPERMAN SLEEP--

"--HIS NIGHTMARES WILL ONLY GROW WORSE UPON HIS AWAKENING!"
HUH? WHAT--WHERE AM I?
GREAT KRYPTON...
LISTEN TO ME, LUTHOR! YOU'RE A FOOL TO TRUST DARKSEID, WHATEVER YOUR AGREEMENT IS--
AND YOU'RE A FOOL IF YOU THINK YOU'RE IN ANY POSITION TO TELL ME WHAT TO DO! OH, AND BY THE WAY, THE HEAT VISION THING IS A DEFINITE NO-NO. THOSE GOGGLES OF DESAAD'S WILL ONLY REFLECT THE BEAMS BACK INTO YOUR RETINAS!
I AM FULL OF NASTY TRICKS, AREN'T I?
OUR AGREEMENT IS SIMPLE. DARKSEID OBTAINS THE SERVICES OF MS. WILLIS HERE, AND IN EXCHANGE, I RECEIVE APOKOLIPS WEAPONS TECHNOLOGY.
YES, YOU SEE, THE CANNON CANNOT FUNCTION SAFELY WITHOUT HER UNIQUE 'ABILITIES!

AH, ALL AWAKE AND AWE-INSPIRED, EH, SUPERMAN? AND WHY NOT? AFTER ALL, IT'S NOT EVERY DAY ONE FINDS ONE-SELF STRAPPED TO THE BARREL OF THE MOST MAGNIFICENT WEAPON OF MASS DESTRUCTION IN THE KNOWN UNIVERSE--
A LITTLE MARVEL OF MILITARY WICKEDNESS I CALL THE ARMAGEDDON CANNON!!
"THE CANNON DRAWS POWER DIRECTLY FROM THE FURNACES OF APOKOLIPS. WE NEED LIVEWIRE TO ACT AS A SORT OF TRANSFORMER-- HER INNATE ABILITY TO CONTROL ENERGY WILL ALLOW US TO STABILIZE THE WEAPON WHILE TAPPING SUCH A MASSIVE POWER SOURCE!
"THE DESTRUCTIVE ENERGY WILL THEN BE FIRED FROM THE CANNON INTO A BOOM TUBE, ALLOWING THE PLANET-BUSTING BLAST TO BE TELEPORTED ANYWHERE IN THE COSMOS!"
SUCH POWER WILL ALLOW US TO SUBDUE OUR ENEMIES ON NEW GENESIS WITHOUT LAUNCHING EVEN A SINGLE OFFENSIVE!

THIS ISN'T OVER YET, DESAAD! LESLIE! CAN YOU HEAR ME? LIVE-WIRE!

HAHAHA! DON'T WASTE YOUR SUPER-BREATH!

MY MENTAL-DAMPENING DEVICES HAVE REDUCED HER TO A COG IN THE MACHINE THAT KNOWS NOTHING SAVE "ON" AND "OFF"!
SELLING LESLIE OUT TO THESE MONSTERS IS A NEW LOW EVEN FOR YOU, LUTHOR!
HOW CAN YOU GO ALONG WITH THIS INSANITY?

STRICTLY BUSINESS, MY FRIEND. I DON'T TELL MY CLIENTS ON EARTH WHAT TO DO WITH THE WEAPONS I SELL THEM. DARKSEID'S WAR WITH NEW GENESIS IS NONE OF MY CONCERN.

ALL I CARE ABOUT--AFTER SEEING YOU "OFF", OF COURSE--IS RETURNING TO EARTH TO REAP THE BENEFITS OF MY DEAL WITH DARKSEID.

WHAT EARTH?
EARTH?

WHAT DO YOU MEAN, "WHAT EARTH?"
PRIMITIVE! HOW DARE YOU ADDRESS LORD DARKSEID IN THAT MANNER?
CONTROL YOUR BLOOD LUST, WILD ONE. LEX LUTHOR HAS DONE MUCH FOR APOKOLIPS THIS DAY AND HE DESERVES AN EXPLANATION!

YOU SEE, LUTHOR, WE ARE HERE TO WITNESS A TEST-FIRING OF THE ARMAGEDDON CANNON. THE TARGET IS A PALTRY PLANET THAT HAS PROVEN BOTHERSOME TO ME IN THE PAST. AN ANNOYING SPECK OF SAND CALLED--THE EARTH!
AND SUPERMAN WILL BE THE FIRST TO FEEL THE CANNON'S FURY BEFORE THE BLAST APPEARS IN THE HEART OF HIS BELOVED METROPOLIS!

I ASSUME THIS WASN'T HOW YOU EXPECTED YOUR BUSINESS ARRANGEMENT TO WORK OUT, LEX...

B-BUT LORD DARKSEID-- THIS WAS NOT PART OF OUR BARGAIN!
YOU'RE GETTING EXACTLY WHAT YOU ASKED FOR, LUTHOR --OUR TECHNOLOGY, WITH SUPERMAN'S DEMISE AS A BONUS. YOU SHOULD BE PLEASED.
A-ARE YOU MAD? HOW ON EARTH AM I SUPPOSED TO USE THE TECHNOLOGY IF--
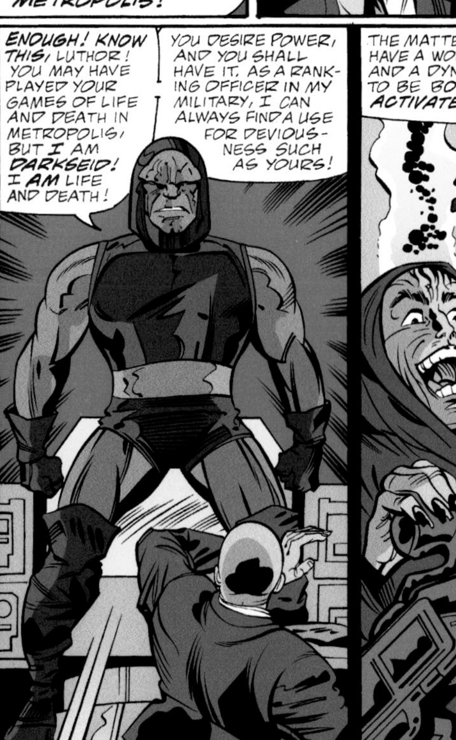
ENOUGH! KNOW THIS, LUTHOR! YOU MAY HAVE PLAYED YOUR GAMES OF LIFE AND DEATH IN METROPOLIS, BUT I AM DARKSEID! I AM LIFE AND DEATH!
YOU DESIRE POWER, AND YOU SHALL HAVE IT. AS A RANKING OFFICER IN MY MILITARY, I CAN ALWAYS FIND A USE FOR DEVIOUSNESS SUCH AS YOURS!

THE MATTER IS ENDED. I HAVE A WORLD TO DESTROY AND A DYNASTY BEGGING TO BE BORN. DESAAD! ACTIVATE THE CANNON!
AT ONCE, LORD DARKSEID!
DON'T THINK OF IT AS LOSING A HOMEWORLD, LUTHOR. THINK OF IT AS GAINING THE UNIVERSE. A MAN WITH A COLD HEART CAN GO FAR ON APOKOLIPS.
YES... I CAN SEE THAT.
COMMENCE ENERGY INTAKE! OPEN THE FLOODGATES TO THE CANNON! LONG LIVE DARKSEID! DEATH TO THE EARTH!

LOOK! THE LIFEBLOOD OF APOKOLIPS ITSELF FLOWS INTO THE CANNON, JUST BEGGING TO REACH OUT AND OBLITERATE THAT FILTHY TERRAN BALL OF MUD!
YES, BUT ONLY IF LIVEWIRE'S POWERS CAN STABILIZE THE ENERGY!
SH-SHH-SHOOOOM!
THROOM!
NNNGGHH...
IT'S WORKING! THE BRAT'S INSTINCTIVELY CHANNELING THE PIT ENERGY--THE CANNON IS HOLDING STEADY!
NOW--OPEN THE BOOM TUBE! DESTINATION--METROPOLIS!
BOOM!
HAPPY NOW, LEX? BAD ENOUGH YOU SOLD LESLIE OUT, NOW YOU'RE GOING TO JUST SIT AND WATCH YOUR HOMEWORLD GET WIPED OUT AS A RESULT?!
YOU'VE NEVER BEEN ONE TO TAKE ORDERS. HOW CAN YOU JUST STAND THERE AND COLDLY LET THIS HAPPEN?
BECAUSE UNLIKE YOU, SUPERMAN, HE UNDERSTANDS TRUE POWER WHEN HE SEES IT. AND BESIDES... IF A "SUPER-MAN" COULDN'T STOP US, WHAT THEN COULD A SIMPLE, ORDINARY MAN DO?
WELL, HE COULD ALWAYS DO SOMETHING LIKE--
--THIS!
LUTHOR--WHAT ARE YOU DOING?!
STOP HIM! HE HAS A SLAYMORE!
LET'S JUST SAY I'M BACKING OUT OF OUR LITTLE BUSINESS AGREEMENT!
NOOOO! NOT THE CANNON CONTROLS, YOU--

BUH-THOOM!
HUH ?! WH-WHERE AM I-- ?
FRZZAT!
SPAKK!
SHUT DOWN THE ENERGY IN-TAKE! QUICKLY, YOU DOGS, WE MUST STABILIZE THE CANNON!
LUTHOR, YOU FOOL! DO YOU REALIZE WHAT YOU'VE DONE ?
ACTUALLY, KANTO, I BELIEVE I'VE JUST SAVED MY HOME PLANET, WITH, I MIGHT ADD, ONE OF YOUR OWN SLAYMORE EX-PLOSIVES, WHICH I POCKETED AFTER YOUR DEFEAT IN METROPOLIS!
YOU'RE MISTAKEN IF YOU THINK YOU'VE ACHIEVED ANYTHING, LUTHOR! WE STILL HAVE THE GIRL, AND THE CANNON WILL BE REPAIRED!
YOU MADE THE MISTAKE WHEN YOU UNDERESTIMATED ME, DARKSEID!
YOU MAY BE LIFE AND DEATH, BUT I'M A BUSINESSMAN-- AND I ALWAYS HAVE A BACKUP PLAN IN CASE ANYONE TRIES TO DOUBLE-CROSS ME!
AND HERE'S ANOTHER THING YOU DIDN'T COUNT ON, "OH GREAT DARKSEID"-- I'D RATHER RULE IN METROPOLIS THAN SERVE ON APOKOLIPS!
YOU'LL DO NEITHER, KALI-BAK--PAY THE MAN FOR HIS TREACHERY!
STUPID EARTH WORM! THAT SLAY-MORE WON'T PREVENT ME FROM POUNDING YOUR PUNY FLESH INTO JELLY!
B-BUT...≡CHOKE!≡ H-HAVEN'T YOU FORGOTTEN ABOUT S-SUPERMAN ?
HA! AND HOW CAN THAT WEAKLING SAVE YOU--
--WHEN HE'S STRAPPED HELPLESSLY TO THE BARREL OF THE ARMA-GEDDON--
--CANNON--?

NO HARD FEELINGS, TOUGH GUY--
--JUST CONSIDER THIS A LITTLE SOMETHING I OWE YOU FROM BEFORE!
KRANG!
WHAT TOOK YOU SO LONG, ALIEN? I WAS NEARLY WORRIED THERE FOR A MINUTE--
DON'T PUSH IT, LEX. I BARELY HAD THE STRENGTH TO BREAK FREE FROM THE CANNON, EVEN AFTER THE POWER LOCKS FAILED ON THE RESTRAINTS.
BESIDES--
--WE'RE NOT OUT OF THIS YET.
WARRIORS OF APOKOLIPS! STAND BACK!
THE TIME IS PAST FOR MERE IRON AND MUSCLE! THIS FOLLY DEMANDS A NEAT AND QUICK RESOLUTION--ONE THAT CAN ONLY BE PROVIDED BY DARKSEID'S DREADED OMEGA EFFECT!
BEHOLD! WITH BUT A GLANCE I WILL REMOVE THESE TWO STAINS FROM MY SIGHT AS IF THEY HAD NEVER EXISTED!
RRRUUMBLE
WHAT IS THIS? APOKOLIPS GROANS-- SENDING THE OMEGA BEAMS ASTRAY!
AIIIEEEEE!

IT'S THE CANNON--IT'S OVERLOADING! BUT THAT'S IMPOSSIBLE! WE SHUT THE ENERGY LINES DOWN!
IF YOU SAY SO, DUH-SAD--
--BUT I DECIDED TO RE-OPEN THEM AFTER YOUR COLLAR GIZMO FIZZLED! THAT IS, AFTER I FREED SUPERMAN!
AWWW, WHAT'S THE MATTER, CRATER-FACE? YOU AND YOUR PLAYMATES DON'T LOOK TOO HAPPY TO SEE ME! I MEAN, ISN'T THIS WHAT YOU BROUGHT ME HERE FOR--
KWA-THOOOM!
--MORE POWER TO YA!!
ZZKRA-KA-KOOOM!
ZRA-KOOM!
KRRUMBLE!
AIEEE! THE GREAT STATUE CRUMBLES! SURELY IT'S A SIGN!
APOKOLIPS IS DOOMED! SAVE US, DARKSEID! SAVE US!
UNBELIEVABLE--SHE'S EXTRACTING ENERGY DIRECTLY FROM APOKOLIPS--
--AND TURNING IT BACK ON THE ENTIRE PLANET!
AND US, YOU IDIOT! ISN'T THIS RICH? TO MEET MY END ON THIS GODFORSAKEN WORLD!
AND WITH YOU AND THAT WILLIS LUNATIC OF ALL PEOPLE!

YOU MAKE A ROTTEN MARTYR, LEX. BUT DON'T WORRY, YOU'RE NOT GOING DOWN WITH THIS PARTICULAR SHIP!
WAIT! WHAT ARE YOU DOING?!
SENDING YOU HOME THROUGH THAT BOOM TUBE STILL SET FOR METROPOLIS--AGAINST MY BETTER JUDGMENT, I MIGHT ADD!
AAAAAGH!
COME ON! WE DON'T HAVE MUCH TIME!
NO CAN DO, BLUE! I'M STAYING RIGHT HERE! THIS CRAZY ALIEN ENERGY'S GOT ME ALL LIT UP LIKE VETERAN'S SQUARE ON NEW YEAR'S EVE--
--AN' I DON'T WANT NOBODY HURT WHEN I GO KABLOOEY EXCEPT FOR THESE BUMS! GET OUT OF HERE WHILE YOU STILL CAN!
SORRY, LESLIE, BUT I CAN'T DO THAT.
OH, YOU BIG DOPE! I KNEW YOU WERE GONNA SAY SOMETHING STUPID LIKE THAT! PUT ME DOWN, I DON'T WANNA FRY YOU, I WANNA FRY THEM!
THEY'RE GETTING AWAY! CLOSE THE TUBE!
LET THEM GO!
THE UNSTABLE PIT ENERGY SHE'S DRAINED WILL SOON DISCHARGE, DOOMING ALL THOSE NEAR HER! LET HIM TAKE THE GIRL AS FAR AWAY AS POSSIBLE--
--SO THAT WE MAY RE-BUILD AND PLAN FOR ANOTHER DAY--
BOOM!

"--WHILE SUPERMAN'S BELOVED METROPOLIS SUFFERS IN FLAMES FROM HIS NAIVE ACT OF HEROISM!"
LOOK! HERE COMES SOMEONE ELSE!
IT'S SUPERMAN--WITH LIVEWIRE! BUT--WHAT'S HAPPENED TO HER?!
EVERYONE, GET BACK! CLEAR THE AREA!
BOOM!
ARE YOU INSANE? HOW COULD YOU BRING THAT HUMAN POWDER KEG HERE TO ENDANGER US ALL? IS THIS HOW YOU REPAY MY SACRIFICE ON APOKOLIPS?
YOU ONLY ACTED TO SAVE YOUR OWN SKIN, LEX, NOT TO MENTION YOUR PATHETIC PRIDE. IF ANYONE WAS WILLING TO SACRIFICE HERSELF UP THERE, IT WAS THIS GIRL YOU PRETENDED TO BEFRIEND.
P-PLEASE... IF IT'S THE LAST THING I DO... L-LEMME FRY THAT CUEBALL...
MAYBE LATER, LESLIE--
--RIGHT NOW I HAVE TO GET YOU AS FAR AWAY FROM HERE AS I CAN BEFORE THE ENERGY YOU'RE CARRYING OVERLOADS. DON'T WORRY, THERE'S A CHANCE YOUR UNIQUE PHYSIOLOGY WILL LET IT PASS THROUGH YOU WITHOUT ANY HARM DONE.
YEAH, BUT WHAT ABOUT YOU, YOU NUMBSKULL? YOU COULD HAVE LEFT ME ON APOKOLIPS LIKE THE MENACE TO SOCIETY THAT I AM--
--INSTEAD, NOW YOU'LL BE TOAST WHEN I GO OFF LIKE A ROMAN CANDLE!
WHAT IS IT WITH YOU AND THIS SAVING EVERYONE STUFF, ANYWAY?
LET'S JUST SAY I BELIEVE I WAS GIVEN MY POWERS TO HELP OTHERS. WHAT'S YOUR STORY?
HUH?
WELL, YOU'VE HELPED SAVE THE EARTH TWICE NOW. PRETTY ODD FOR A "MENACE TO SOCIETY."
OH, THAT. MAYBE I'M SICK OR SOMETHING, OR MAYBE I JUST DON'T WANNA BE A RAT LIKE LEX LUTHOR ALL MY LIFE.
DON'T GET ANY FUNNY IDEAS ABOUT YOUR NAUSEATING LITTLE BOY SCOUT ACT RUBBIN' OFF ON ME. GOT ME?
DON'T WORRY. I'VE GOT YOU...

H-HE'S NOT BREATHING-- AND I CAN'T HEAR A HEARTBEAT!

AW, MAN. YOU GOTTA BE KIDDING ME-- THIS CAN'T BE HAPPENING!

I GOTTA DO SOMETHING--BUT WHAT?
I KNOW! THOSE MEDICAL SHOWS ON TV ARE ALWAYS USIN' ELECTRICITY TO START PEOPLE'S HEARTS, ALL THAT STAT-STAT-STAT STUFF! MAYBE I CAN JOLT HIS TICKER INTO RE-TICKING!
CRIPES, I JUST REALIZED-- I DUNNO IF I EVEN HAVE ENOUGH JOLTAGE LEFT IN ME TO DO THIS!
WELL, I GUESS THERE'S ONLY ONE WAY TO FIND OUT!
THIS HAD BETTER WORK! OTHERWISE MILLIONS OF CRYING KIDS WILL BE AFTER ME FOR THE REST OF MY LIFE!
C'MON! OH, PLEASE, C'MON --
BZZRAAAT!
ZAKK!
WELL, PLUG ME IN AND CALL ME A LIGHTBULB! I DID IT! HE'S GOT A TRIPHAMMER AN' EVERYTHING!
L-LIVEWIRE... YOU--
YEAH, YEAH, I SAVED YOU... DON'T REMIND ME, Y'BIG BLUE HAYSEED. AND YOU MIGHT AS WELL CALL ME LESLIE FROM NOW ON--
--'CAUSE I THINK THIS LI'L OL' FUSEBOX IS BURNT OUT FOR GOOD.

--SUPERMAN AND MS. WILLIS WERE BOTH TREATED AT S.T.A.R. LABS AND RELEASED EARLIER TODAY WITH A CLEAN BILL OF HEALTH.
HOWEVER, ACCORDING TO S.T.A.R., THE ALIEN ENERGY OVERLOAD APPARENTLY SHORTED OUT LESLIE'S LIVEWIRE ABILITIES.
TEEN
AND WHILE WILLIS WOULDN'T COMMENT ON WHY SHE'S BROKEN WITH HER FORMER BENEFACTOR LEX LUTHOR AFTER YESTERDAY'S EVENTS, SHE DID HAVE THIS TO SAY REGARDING THE LOSS OF HER ELECTRICAL ABILITIES...
ACTUALLY, AFTER THIS, I'M KIND OF GLAD I LOST THEM.
I MEAN, SUPER POWERS ARE OKAY, BUT NOW I CAN GET ON WITH MY LIFE AS AN EVERYDAY, NORMAL PERSON.
Y'KNOW, I USED TO THINK SHE WAS JUST A BIG-MOUTHED TROUBLE MAKER, BUT THAT WILLIS TURNED OUT TO BE PRETTY ALL RIGHT.
MAYBE SUPERMAN WAS A GOOD INFLUENCE ON HER, EH, CLARK? HEY, CLARK?
DAILY PLANET
SUPERMAN AND LIVEWIRE SAVE EARTH AGAIN!

"LESLIE TOLD THIS REPORTER SHE PLANS TO LEAVE OUR FAIR CITY AND START OVER IN HER HOME TOWN OF GOTHAM CITY. I'M SURE ALL OF METROPOLIS WISHES HER ALL THE LUCK IN THE WORLD WITH HER NEW LIFE!"
OH, THIS IS JUST GREAT! THE BATTERY'S DEAD! LOUSY RENTAL CAR!

AND TO THINK, A FEW HOURS AGO I COULD'VE JUST KISSED THE IGNITION AND BAM! GOOD TO GO! OR HECK, I COULD'VE JUST FLOWN AWAY!
NOW I'LL HAVE TO WALK BACK TO METROP-OLIS, JUST LIKE ANY OTHER POOR SLOB STUCK OUT HERE IN ALL THIS RAIN AND--

--LIGHTNING...
B-BOOOM!

AWW, NO, NOT THAT! DON'T EVEN THINK IT, LESLIE GIRL! YOU'RE ALL DONE WITH THAT JOLT JAZZ, RIGHT? RIGHT?

WRONG!

H-HEY UP THERE! YOU RE-MEMBER ME, DON'TCHA?! LESLIE WILLIS? SUPERMAN INTRODUCED US A LITTLE WHILE BACK, 'MEMBER? WELL, LOOK, I COULD REALLY USE A LITTLE RECHARGE HERE.
SO, LIKE, WHADDAYA SAY?!

OH, COME ON NOW, DON'T BE SHY! IT'S ME--

--L-L-LIVEWIRE!
ZZZAAKT!

OH, YOU REMEMBERED! OH, THANK YOU! THANK YOU!
HA HA HA! I GUESS LIGHTNING REALLY CAN STRIKE TWICE!

WELL, S'LONG, METROPOLIS! AND LATER FOR YOU, APOKOLIPS! DON'T WORRY, I'LL BE IN TOUCH!
IN THE MEANTIME, SEE YA IN THE FUNNY-PAPERS!
HA HA HA HA HA!
LIGHTS OUT, KIDS!

Want more diabolical scheming and villainy?
Don't miss out on Superman and Lex Luthor's first meeting in *Superman of Smallville*!

LATER, ON THE KENT FARM...

RAKE
RAKE

HI, PA!
HI, CLARK!
HOW WAS SCHOOL?

IT WAS OKAY.
JUST OKAY?

I MADE THE WRESTLING TEAM.
THERE YOU GO!
I KNEW YOU COULD DO IT!

NOW, GO CHANGE INTO YOUR WORK CLOTHES...
WE HAVE CHORES...

...TO FINISH.

CUTE.
NOW, CLARK, REMEMBER...

... NO POWERS DURING YOUR CHORES.
OKAY, PA.

A GOOD HONEST DAY'S WORK IS THE KEY TO A GOOD FOUNDATION IN LIFE.

OKAY, CLARK. PUT THE COWS IN THE BARN.
I'LL BE RIGHT BACK.

REMEMBER, SON...
...NO POWERS!

OKAY, COWS.
LET'S GO!

IN THE BARN, COWS.
C'MON, TIME TO GO.

UM...
LET'S GO, LADIES...
...IN THE BARN!

HMM. MAYBE JUST A LITTLE BIT OF SUPERPOWER WILL HELP.

Moo!
MOO!
MOO!

LIFT

DROP

SLAM!

BRUSH
CLAP
CLAP

CLARK!

UM...

...CLARK.

DO IT AGAIN.

THE RIGHT WAY.

PLEASE.

MUCH LATER...
SO, YOU FLOAT?
YEAH.
IT SEEMS LIKE ANYTIME I'M AROUND LANA, MY POWERS GO CRAZY.
SHE'S A GOOD FRIEND, ISN'T SHE?

YES, OF COURSE! SHE'S AWESOME!

AND YOU FEEL VERY COMFORTABLE AROUND HER, DON'T YOU?
YEAH!
A GOOD FRIEND CAN MAKE YOU FEEL HAPPY.
SHE'S MY BEST FRIEND!

YES, YES.
AND WHEN YOU FEEL CONTENT OR COMFORTABLE OR HAPPY...
...CLARK...
...YOU FLOAT.
YOU ALWAYS HAVE.

CHOMP!
BANANA CREAM PUDDING WOULD DO WONDERS.
MMMMM...

I STILL LOVE BANANA CREAM.

HA.
TELL ME MORE ABOUT THAT WRESTLING TEAM.

ACROSS TOWN...
LUTHOR

WHO
IS
SUPERMAN
?

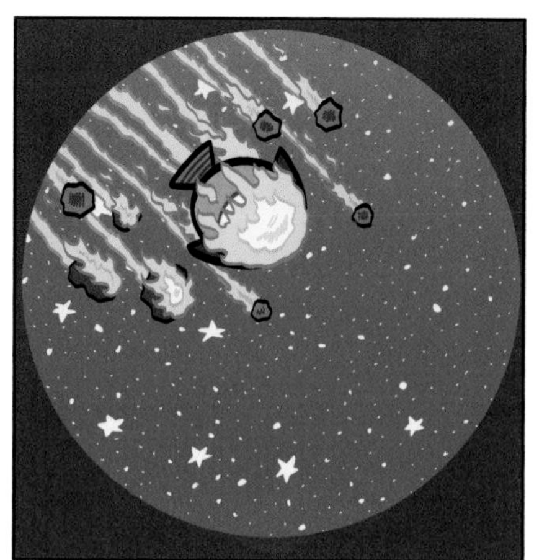

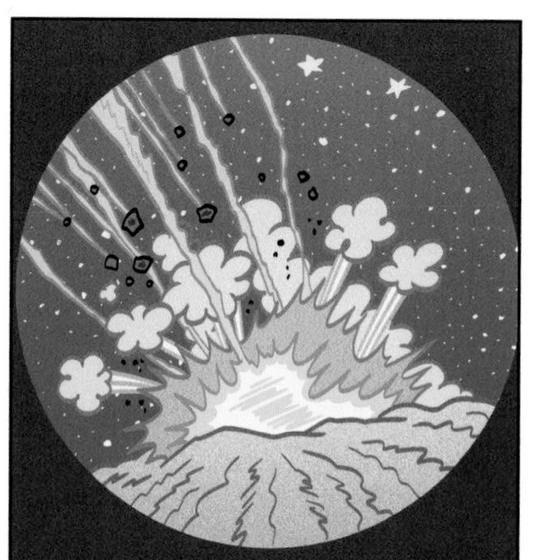

Continued in SUPERMAN of Smallville